Josh had wanted
and now she was

Paige didn't stop him when he slowly urged her legs apart. She didn't object when he lowered his mouth and nuzzled her, drawing deeply of her scent and slicking his thumb over petal-soft folds. She didn't protest when his tongue stroked her intimately. She simply closed her eyes and sighed. There were no barriers between them, no restrictions.

It didn't take her long to find a shattering release. She shuddered and arched. "Josh, come inside me," she whispered.

She was ready for him and he couldn't wait a second longer. After the first deep thrust, her body softened around him, accepting him, enveloping him so that he couldn't tell where he ended and she began. With a rough groan, he gave her the wild ride she wanted.

He felt the first tiny quiver of release convulse around him, heard a sob break from her throat along with his name. He opened his eyes and looked down just in time to see the pleasure on her face. That's all it took. His own climax slammed into him, powerful and unrelenting. Never had he experienced such fire, such passion...or the primal need to possess.

But then he'd never loved a woman the way he loved Paige.

Dear Reader,

Have you ever wanted something that was unattainable? Something almost forbidden? Most of us have. For Detective Josh Marchiano, that something has always been his best friend's wife, Paige Montgomery. But now, Anthony Montgomery is dead, and Josh is assigned to protect Paige from a ruthless man who believes she has the diamond-and-emerald necklace her husband had stolen!

Protecting Paige has its advantages, especially when Josh must pose as her lover and live with her. But Paige is more stubborn than Josh expected, and it takes more than a few sexy kisses and seductive caresses to make her believe they can live happily ever after.

I hope you enjoy Paige and Josh's story. If you'd like to know what other titles I have upcoming with Temptation, you can check out my web page by visiting Harlequin's web site (http://www.romance.net) and clicking on my name in the author links, or you can write to me at P.O. Box 1102, Rialto, CA 92377-1102. I look forward to hearing from you!

Happy Reading,

Janelle Denison

Books by Janelle Denison

HARLEQUIN TEMPTATION
679—PRIVATE PLEASURES
682—PRIVATE FANTASIES

FORBIDDEN
Janelle Denison

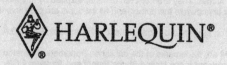

HARLEQUIN®

TORONTO • NEW YORK • LONDON
AMSTERDAM • PARIS • SYDNEY • HAMBURG
STOCKHOLM • ATHENS • TOKYO • MILAN • MADRID
PRAGUE • WARSAW • BUDAPEST • AUCKLAND

A special thanks to Jamie Denton, whose friendship
and belief make each book a reality.
Thank you for your faith in me on this one!
To Karen Drogin, for sending a thank-you note that turned
into something far more special. I treasure your friendship.
And, as always, to my husband, Don, who is the reason why
writing romance, and creating sexy, good-guy
heroes comes so easily to me.

ISBN 0-373-25832-1

FORBIDDEN

Look us up on-line at: http://www.romance.net

Printed in U.S.A.

PAIGE MONTGOMERY looked beautiful in black, Josh Marchiano decided. Graceful, elegant and poised, despite the recent tragedy that had made her a widow.

A small, intimate crowd of friends and family filled Paige's luxurious oceanfront home, to offer their condolences after attending the funeral services for her husband, Anthony Montgomery. Josh stood off to the side, near the spread of food the arrivals were contributing to, watching as Paige made sure she greeted everyone. A faint smile touched her lips as she gently squeezed the hand of an elderly woman offering her sympathies. Paige nodded in response to something the woman said, then moved on to the next person.

Sadness dimmed her green eyes. That particular emotion was one Josh had seen too frequently during Paige's three-year marriage to the man he'd once considered his best friend. There had been too many promises Anthony had broken, too many nights he'd opted to spend out with the boys instead of with the woman waiting for him at home.

Anthony had treated Paige more like a possession than a wife, and over the years Josh had found himself trying to make up for Anthony's neglect by being a friend to Paige. His good intentions had backfired.

Anthony might have married Paige, but Josh had fallen in love with her.

Paige glanced around, as if searching for someone

specific, and stopped when she saw him. From across the room their gazes connected. Her expression softened, and for several heartbeats everyone else in the room faded away. A familiar awareness stirred between them, a tempting attraction neither one of them had ever talked about, or acted upon.

It didn't make the chemistry between them any less powerful.

She started toward him, weaving through the guests. Her simple, traditional black dress draped subtly along her slender curves to just above the knee. Smoke-hued stockings encased a pair of long legs down to black heels. The dark color accentuated her flawless complexion and complemented her hair, a rich brown shade with natural auburn highlights. Today, she'd worn her hair up in an efficient, neat twist. Josh had the fleeting thought that he preferred the thick, silky strands flowing free down around her shoulders.

She stopped in front of him, her gaze at once uncertain and expectant. Not caring that there were people in the room, Josh closed the distance between them and brushed his lips across her cheek.

"I'm so sorry, Paige," he said, knowing he'd repeated that sentiment at least a hundred times since delivering the devastating news of Anthony's death. The condolence seemed inadequate in view of the tragic events of the past week.

"Yeah, me too," she whispered, a wealth of heartache lingering in her soft voice. "Thanks for coming today."

"You don't need polite formalities with me." Frowning at her, he pushed back his suit jacket and slid his hands into the front pockets of his navy trousers. "You know I would have been here for you. No matter what."

Her smile didn't reach her eyes. "I wasn't sure if your lieutenant was going to let you attend the service, considering the risk to the case Anthony was working on."

"Lieutenant Reynolds had no choice in the matter."

Oh, they'd argued vehemently about the possible hazards of a Metro-Dade detective attending the funeral of a man who'd worked undercover to infiltrate a jewel-smuggling ring. In the end, Josh had won the heated debate. Though Anthony had been killed in the line of duty, sources still on the case had reported that no one in the ring had known Anthony Montgomery was a vice cop. He'd died with his assumed identity intact. Lieutenant Reynolds had decided any police association or political fanfare normally accompanying the death of a law enforcement officer would only draw attention to Anthony's true occupation and risk the lives of the other undercover officers still planted in the ring, so his funeral had become a simple, intimate affair, without any pomp and circumstance.

Josh had suggested that one ordinary person could blend in with family and friends much easier than a hundred uniformed officers. His lieutenant grudgingly agreed that it might not be a bad idea if he kept an eye on Paige until things settled down, and they determined the motive for Anthony's death.

"I could really use some fresh air," Paige said, pulling Josh's thoughts off police bureaucracy and back to her. "Care to join me?"

Considering how claustrophobic the house was beginning to feel, the thought of sunshine and a cool breeze appealed to him. "Sure."

He had every intention of passing through the living room to the slider leading to the deck where other peo-

ple had gathered, but she grabbed his arm before he
could head that way.

"I want to be alone," she said, answering his ques-
tioning look. "If we go that way it'll take me an hour of
accepting more condolences before we make it out to
the deck, and it's even getting crowded out there."

He smiled, understanding she was tired of keeping
up a polite front. "Come on, we'll sneak out the other
way." Pressing his hand to the small of her back, he
ushered her toward the marbled foyer.

They slipped discreetly out the front door and followed a tiled walkway veering toward the right side of
the house. The path led to a white gazebo surrounded
by tropical plants and flowers. Night-blooming jasmine
twined through the lattice columns around the structure. The warmth of the mild fall afternoon intensified
the pleasant fragrance drifting from the tiny white
flowers.

Once inside the gazebo, Paige crossed to the opening
overlooking a stretch of Miami beach and the Atlantic
Ocean beyond. Pressing her hands to the railing, she
took a deep breath of sea air. Josh imagined he could
see some of her tension drain away.

"How have you been?" he asked quietly. He'd asked
her that question numerous times over the past week
when he'd talked to her on the phone and always received an automatic response of "fine." In person, he
expected a more honest answer.

She didn't disappoint him. Glancing back at him, she
gave a slight shrug. "As well as can be expected, I suppose. I'm glad the funeral is over, but I have to admit
that Anthony's death still doesn't seem real."

What with the funeral arrangements, the steady
stream of people paying their respects, and the arrival

of her sister, Valerie, from Connecticut offering moral support, he guessed she'd been too distracted to accept the reality of the situation. "It'll take more than a week for the shock to wear off, Paige."

"Oh, the sensible side of me knows that," she said, leaning against one of the jasmine-draped columns. "But Anthony was gone so much that a part of me just feels like this is an extended leave on another case."

He heard the pain in her voice that touched beyond her current sorrow. It mingled with the misery and loneliness he'd seen glimpses of the past few years, and grabbed at something deep and elemental in him.

Folding her arms across her chest, she turned her gaze back out to the sea. "You know, it was one of my greatest fears that Anthony would get killed working on some secretive, undercover case."

"Getting killed in the line of duty is a risk all cops take." He grimaced. The automatic response sounded trite even to his own ears.

"Yeah, Anthony told me that plenty of times," she said, her lips pursing into a tight, angry line. "It never did do much to ease the fears and uncertainties or the long, sleepless nights."

"I'm sorry." He didn't know what else to say.

"Don't be." She waved a hand in the air as if to dismiss his apology. "You know, his occupation was a bone of contention in our marriage. He loved the risk of undercover work, the thrill of the danger that went with it. I grew to hate it."

By the look in her eyes, she'd despised his occupation for more reasons than she'd ever divulged to him. "It's not always easy being a cop's wife."

She tilted her head and regarded him speculatively. "Why didn't you warn me before I married one?"

Recognizing the teasing sparkle in her eyes, he allowed a slow grin to lift the corners of his mouth. "Would you have listened?"

She laughed, the breezy sound breaking the tension caused by their previous conversation. "Probably not."

The lighthearted moment reminded him why he enjoyed her company so much. "Then there's your answer."

She shook her head, and picked at one of the little white flowers, her face serious again. "Have you learned any more about the accident that killed him?"

He chose his answer carefully, not wanting to divulge any of the disturbing suspicions circulating about Anthony's death being more than just an accident. "It's still under investigation."

"And it's confidential information," she added for him, bitterness creeping back into her voice.

He sighed heavily, wondering how many times she'd heard that same line from her own husband. "Yes, it is."

She flicked the flower over the rail and watched it flutter to the landscaped lawn. "Well, when you're at liberty to share the privileged information, I'd like some answers on what, exactly, happened."

He nodded. Giving her closure was the least he could do for her. "As soon as the investigation is concluded, and the reports released, I'll let you know."

And for Paige's sake as much as his own, he hoped the rumors of criminal involvement surrounding Anthony were unfounded.

1

Three months later

JOSH GLANCED out the windshield of his black Thunderbird and scowled at the thick, gray clouds overhead. The dreary, temperamental weather settling over North Miami Beach suited his mood, which was grim, with an angry undercurrent as ferocious as the jagged bolts of lightning streaking across the darkening sky. The elements of the brewing storm about to break weren't much different from the sense of betrayal raging within him.

Shifting his gaze to the luxurious, custom-built home he'd parked in front of, he attempted to push his surly emotions aside so he could mentally prepare himself for the unpleasant task ahead. Not easy, considering his personal feelings for the woman inside that house.

Paige.

Dread settled in his chest, and he scrubbed both hands over his face, feeling the burn of his two-day stubble against his palms. It had been that long since Lieutenant Reynolds had summoned him into his office and verified what had been mere speculation among the cops working on the case Anthony had been assigned to. With the help of the officers still working undercover on the case, Internal Affairs had concluded their investigation of the sudden, merciless death of

Anthony Montgomery. The official reports had confirmed the rumors no one in the department, least of all himself, wanted to believe.

Anthony Montgomery had been dirty, and he'd tangled Paige in the middle of the mess. Because of Anthony's deceit, she was about to be dragged into a world where violence and greed reigned.

Josh was her best hope of surviving.

A fresh wave of anger gripped him, and he tightened his fingers on the steering wheel. It outraged and disgusted him that Anthony had stooped low enough to put his own wife into such a dangerous situation.

You were his best friend, Josh, ol' buddy. You knew better than most that Anthony rarely thought of anyone but himself.

Yeah, he'd seen that selfish, arrogant side of Anthony many times in the years since they'd graduated from the Academy together, but he'd believed marriage to someone as gentle and caring as Paige would tame and humble him. Not so. If anything, Anthony had grown more cocky and reckless. His last actions on earth proved his disregard for the wife he'd left behind.

Tamping down the flare of emotions, Josh flipped up the collar of his lightweight jacket, slid out of the vehicle and headed toward the front of Paige's house. Thunder shook the heavens, and the wind began to howl and whip through the nearby palms and trees. Then the sky split wide open, and big, fat drops of rain began to fall. Within seconds, he was drenched.

With a distinct curse, he leapt onto the tile steps and ducked under the awning covering the front porch, which sheltered him from the pelting rain and wild winds.

"Great," he muttered. Dragging his fingers through

his wet hair, he pushed the thick, unruly strands into some semblance of order. His face was wet, too, the excess moisture trailing down his neck and into the collar of his shirt. "Just great."

Puffing out an aggravated breath, he knocked firmly on the heavy oak door. Through the etched-glass insets he could see the soft glow of lights illuminating portions of the house, then a slim, blurred figure moving toward the foyer. A lock unlatched, then the door opened.

"Josh!" Paige smiled, surprise and pleasure brightening her striking green eyes. "What are you doing here?"

Recent revelations caused his fierce protective instincts to rise swiftly to the surface. "Do you always open the door to strangers without asking who's standing on the other side?"

She blinked, taken aback by his abrupt question. "You're hardly a stranger, Josh."

He resisted the urge to reach out and shake her. "You didn't know it was me when you opened the door."

A dark auburn brow lifted, and she crossed her arms over her chest. She looked nice and cozy and *dry*, Josh noted grumpily, taking in her cocoa-colored knit sweater that hung to mid-thigh, and slim leggings in the same shade. Her feet were bare, though, her toenails a light shade of pink. And her hair was down, a thick luxurious tumble of cinnamon and fire. The tips of his cold fingers tingled at the thought of burying them in such silky, sensual warmth.

"If the purpose of your visit is a lecture, Detective Marchiano, I don't need it."

"Seems to me you do." He scowled at her for being so

naive, and at himself for letting his mind drift to other forbidden enticements. "You're too damn trusting."

Before the night was over, though, he was going to shatter that guileless trust of hers, the serenity of her life, and make her suspicious of everyone she came into contact with.

The way she viewed the world would never be the same.

"It's a trait some people appreciate," she replied lightly.

"And others take advantage of." The tail end of a gust found its way into his corner of the porch. A chill shivered throughout his body and made goose bumps rise on his damp flesh. The glowing warmth of her house beckoned.

"You know, Josh, you look like hell, and you're as surly as an angry bear." She tilted her head, regarding him with a small degree of amusement. "If you're looking for me to invite you in, you're going about it the wrong way."

If he'd been standing on her doorstep under different circumstances, he would have laughed. His relationship with Paige had always included plenty of good-natured teasing, and the smiles and laughter that seemed to be lacking in her relationship with Anthony. They'd always gotten along well—too well, he sometimes thought, connecting on so many levels that stretched beyond simple friendship.

Today, laughter wasn't on the agenda. Instead, he blew out a harsh breath that did nothing to ease the anxiety knotting up his insides. "This isn't a social call," he said, his tone heavy with regret. "I'm here on official business."

"Oh." Her smile fell away, as did the tenderness and

teasing. She automatically stepped aside to let him enter.

He brushed past her and into the foyer, welcoming the rise in temperature. The interior of the house was warm and inviting, redolent with the pleasing aroma of fresh-baked bread and another richer scent he couldn't name, but his empty stomach appreciated nonetheless.

He stopped just inside the entryway, when the soles of his leather loafers squeaked against marble. Not wanting to muddy the expensive Oriental runner leading to the living room, he toed his shoes off by the door.

"Criminy," he muttered, shaking his head in disgust. "Even my socks are wet." He took those off, too, and put them with his shoes.

Paige tried to smother a grin, and failed. "You're absolutely soaked, Josh."

He jammed his hands on his hips and glanced down at himself. There wasn't a dry patch on his jacket, and his jeans were plastered to his hips and legs. The wet denim was heavy and clammy against his skin. "Right down to my briefs," he confirmed wryly. "I got caught in the downpour."

"Let me get you a towel."

She left him standing in the foyer, and returned in less than a minute with a fluffy, cream-colored towel. He took it from her and dried his face, then ran its thickness over his dripping hair.

"Why don't you get out of those wet clothes and I'll throw them in the dryer?" she suggested.

He stopped towel-drying his hair and met her gaze. A faint smile quirked the corner of his mouth. "And run around in the buff?"

A lovely shade of pink suffused her face. "No," she said primly. "I haven't cleaned out all of Anthony's stuff yet. I'm sure I've got an extra pair of sweats you can use."

A shiver snaked down his spine, making him all too aware that he was chilled to the bone—and would remain so for hours if he didn't change out of his wet clothes. He'd be no help to Paige if he got sick; she needed him healthy, his mind sharp and his body alert.

"I'd appreciate that." Unzipping his jacket, he shrugged it off and hung it to air-dry on the elegantly carved mahogany coatrack by the door.

Her gaze went to the holster strapped to his left shoulder, and the 9mm Beretta tucked within it, a direct reminder of who and what he was. A cop. His automatic pistol was as much a part of him as his limbs were, a natural extension of his persona as a homicide detective. He rarely left home without it, and it would be his constant companion until this new ordeal was over.

Judging by the aversion glittering in her eyes, she resented that particular intrusion into her home. Her life.

Guilt rippled through him, and he resisted the impulse to reach out and touch her, to offer reassurances. But he couldn't extend false hope. Couldn't dispense with his weapon no matter how much she wanted him to. Not when her life was at stake, and the future so uncertain. She needed to accept his presence, and reconcile herself to the fact that he would protect her with the most persuasive, and lethal, means possible.

Before the night was over, she would understand his purpose, and accept it. She had no choice.

Finally, she turned away, heading toward the main part of the house. "Come on in to the living room where it's warm," she said over her shoulder. "And I'll get you the sweats to change into."

She veered off to the right, disappearing down the hall that led to the master bedroom, a guest room and an office. Josh stepped into the living room and gravitated toward the dying fire in the hearth. He tossed a few more logs on the grate, and absorbed the warmth while his eyes surveyed the room and its rich, luxurious furnishings.

Josh had often wondered how Anthony had been able to afford such an extravagant and somewhat pretentious home on a relatively modest salary. Over the years, Anthony's outrageous spending habits had included custom-made racing boats, fast sports cars and other expensive, frivolous toys. Anthony had always lived life to its fullest, never hesitating before purchasing his newest whim—not before Paige had come into the picture, and certainly not after.

So where had that constant flow of cash come from? Anthony had no wealthy family to back him up, and no inheritance or trust fund drawing interest. In light of recent events, the most logical explanation burned like acid in Josh's stomach.

Soft, relaxing music drifted from the speakers mounted in the corners of the room, and his gaze took in the invoices, files and catalogs spread out on the coffee table. A nearly empty glass of wine sat in the midst of the paperwork.

Investigative instincts prompted him to move closer. He caught the name of Paige's boutique, the Wild Rose, embossed in mauve on cream-hued stationery. A deep green vine and dew-pearled roses trailed across the heading and down the left side. The letter was addressed to a broker, the contents half-covered by another piece of paper with impressive dollar amounts listed.

Frowning, and wondering what kind of business Paige might have with a broker, he reached for the letter.

"Are you looking for something in particular, *Detective?*"

Damn. He casually straightened and glanced at Paige, who stood at the end of the leather couch, sweats in hand, watching him steadily. "Nope." He grinned. "Just admiring your pretty stationery."

A faint smile touched her lips, but didn't reach her eyes. "If I knew you had a penchant for roses and trailing vines, I would have given you your own personalized notepaper for Christmas." Her words were sugarcoated, but not enough to sweeten the sarcasm in her voice.

He shrugged. "Maybe next year."

"Don't play those games with me, Josh," she said, her mouth thinning in anger. "I had enough of them with Anthony."

He had no desire to be compared to her deceased husband. "Fair enough." At that moment, he decided candidness between them was crucial. "I was curious as to why the Wild Rose would be contacting a broker."

She stared at him for a long, hard moment, a range of emotions flitting across her face—none of which were complimentary or reassuring. Finally, she said, "It's none of your business."

He wanted to refute that and demand answers, especially since she was being so vague and secretive. As a friend, he had an interest in her life. She'd certainly never been reticent about information about her flourishing boutique before, so it was even more disturbing that she was now. As the man assigned to protect her, his concern stemmed from that essential need to know all the facts so nothing took him by surprise.

She approached him, dismissing their conversation by handing over the gray cotton sweats. "You're welcome to take a hot shower to get rid of the chill."

He let the subject slide, for now. There were more pressing issues to address than the fate of her boutique. "Thanks. I think I will. I'll be a few minutes, and then we'll talk."

"I can hardly wait," he heard her mutter beneath her breath as he headed out of the room.

DAMN JOSH ANYWAY!

Paige didn't need whatever "official business" he was here to disclose, not when she was desperately trying to get her life back on track. Not when she was so close to making decisions that affected her future. The last thing she needed was more emotional turmoil clouding her judgment.

And a deep, gut instinct warned her that the investigation on Anthony's death had been concluded, and that was the reason for Josh's formal visit.

You're the one who insisted Josh give you answers, a part of her mind chided.

Yeah, well, over the passing three months she'd had a change of heart. Her initial anger over the situation had eased, and she'd managed to bury her resentment of the undercover work her husband had thrived on. Anthony was gone, and nothing anyone could say or do could turn back the clock. Did she really want to know the gory details of why there wasn't enough left of Anthony after the fatal explosion to justify a casket?

No, she didn't.

She'd come to terms with his death, and the choices

he'd made, despite the heartache it had cost her. Now, all she wanted was to put this chapter of her life behind her, and begin anew.

Rubbing the slow throb beginning at her temple, Paige forced herself to regain her composure. It wasn't easy, considering the negative vibes Josh had brought with him today. His tension had been nearly palpable, touching off emotions that made her feel uncomfortably vulnerable.

She knew Josh well, in some ways better than she'd known her own husband. She'd learned to gauge his moods, valued his openness and appreciated his honesty, elements her relationship with Anthony had lacked. During the past year she'd spent more time with Josh than she had with Anthony. Josh didn't realize it, but his friendship and companionship had kept her sane during a very turbulent and emotionally draining marriage.

Anthony hadn't turned out to be the man he'd presented during their whirlwind, three-month courtship. Kindness, tenderness and consideration, the very traits she'd fallen in love with, had waned just months after the wedding. The dreams she'd harbored since she was a little girl had diminished within a year, yet she'd always held on to a small glimmer of hope that things would change...that Anthony would realize just how rich and wonderful having a family could be. That there was more to life than the next exciting undercover case.

A burst of derisive laughter escaped her. She'd been kidding herself. Anthony had been too egotistical to stretch beyond his own wants and needs, and too arrogant and possessive to let her go when there was no incentive for her to remain in a loveless marriage.

Lightning flashed through the glass slider leading to

the deck, and thunder rumbled in the distance, startling her back to the present. Shaking off her unsettling thoughts, she sat on the couch and began clearing the coffee table and putting files back into her briefcase. She would review her paperwork later, after Mr. Inquisitive left.

Picking up her glass of wine, she debated on a refill, then decided that Josh could probably use a cup of coffee, and since she'd be making a pot, she might as well join him. Padding into the kitchen, she filled the carafe with water, then scooped French Vanilla coffee into the basket. While the coffee percolated, she washed the few dinner dishes she'd left in the sink. Once that was done, she found herself staring out the kitchen window to the darkness beyond, trying to think of the best way to tell Josh she no longer had a burning desire to know the details of Anthony's death. That she preferred to remember the few good memories she had of Anthony.

"Ummm. Coffee smells great."

Paige turned at the sound of Josh's deep, rumbling voice, the offer to pour him a cup dying on her lips before it even formed. Her heart did a funny little leap in her chest as he walked toward her, wearing a smile and the sweatpants she'd given him. Nothing else. His chest was bare, its width tightly muscled and sprinkled with a dusting of dark curls that still looked damp from his shower. The trail tapered down a flat, lean belly, whorled around his navel and disappeared into the waistband of his drawstring sweats.

Heat suffused her entire body, a sensual, feminine kind of awareness that made her skin tingle. Her reaction shocked her—she'd seen Josh without a shirt plenty of times, and never had she experienced this deep, coiling need in the pit of her belly. In the summer, he would often come over, lounge around on the beach and swim in the ocean, wearing nothing more than a pair of swimming trunks. But there was something incredibly intimate and sexy about seeing him after a shower, his skin still flushed from the heat of the water, his black hair a silky tumble around his head. The dark stubble lining his jaw intensified the fascinating, rich shade of those brown-gold eyes that at times seemed to mesmerize her.

Like now.

She swallowed, hard. There'd always been a certain attraction between the two of them; she'd be a hypocrite to deny the underlying magnetism to their friendship. But she'd *never* given a thought to pursuing something so forbidden. No matter how strained her relationship with Anthony had been, no matter how lonely she'd been, no matter that Josh had filled that emptiness within her, her marriage vows had been sacred.

Josh had been nothing more than a friend, someone to talk to when she needed to vent, a person who understood her better than her husband because Josh took the time to listen. A companion when Anthony chose work, and even more often play, over the plans she'd made for them.

He'd always been a platonic friend.

Circumstances had changed, and she realized her feelings for him now had intensified—both physically and emotionally. The realization scared the hell out of her. The mere idea of investing emotions in another relationship strained by the pressures, dangers, and stress of working in law enforcement terrified her.

"Where's the sweatshirt?" she blurted, wanting to do

something about the more immediate hazard to her senses.

"It's too small, and I can barely fit it over my head," he said, absently rubbing a hand over that bare chest of his. "The sweatpants aren't quite my size, either, but they'll do."

Her traitorous gaze slid downward, past the waistband of his sweats this time. The soft cotton clinging to his lean hips, muscular thighs, and more masculine anatomy confirmed his claim. The hems of the sweats ended at his shins. Anthony had been shorter than Josh by a few inches, and not nearly so wide across the chest and shoulders.

"I'll go see if I can find a larger shirt that might fit," she said, and started around him.

He caught her arm, gently. The heat of his fingers seeped through the knit of her sweater, tripping old, familiar sensations her body had been denied for too long. She struggled to ignore the physical response, the ache and need that tightened her chest.

"Paige, I'm fine, really." He looked at her oddly, making her realize how extreme her behavior had become. How ridiculous she was being. "The shower took away the chill, and the living room is warm enough. This will do until my clothes are dry."

She forced a bright, everything-is-okay smile. "I'll go put them in the dryer." The sooner he was fully clothed, the better.

"I already did it," he told her, and released her arm.

"Oh." Her voice reflected her surprise. "I would have done it for you."

He chucked her gently beneath the chin, a fond gesture he'd used many times in the past. It brought her back to familiar territory. Friends.

"I know you would have, but I'm perfectly capable of doing it myself." His grin was all Marchiano charm. "Being a bachelor has some merits, one of which is learning to do your own laundry."

Anthony had never learned that particular skill. She doubted he even knew how to operate the fancy, digital washing machine in the laundry room. Before he'd married her, he'd had a housekeeper who'd taken care of washing the day-to-day essentials, and a dry-cleaning service that picked up and delivered other items needing more care.

"Would you like some soup and fresh sourdough bread?" she asked, grabbing at the most logical way to stall the inevitable.

He shook his head, his expression taking a serious turn. "Maybe later."

We need to talk. She read the words in his eyes, knew it was unavoidable. Knew it was time.

"Coffee?"

"Yeah, I could use a cup."

She opened the cupboard next to the sink and brought down two mugs. "Why don't you go put a few more logs on the fire, and I'll be right there?"

"Okay."

He left the kitchen, and moments later she heard a muted "thump," then the snap and crackle of fire licking at fresh wood. Pouring the fresh-brewed coffee into their mugs, she added cream and sugar to hers, and left his black, the way he preferred it. She carried the two cups into the living room and set them on the coffee table.

She'd forgotten about his gun, but Josh obviously hadn't. He'd removed the pistol from his holster, and had placed it on the end table. The dark steel gleamed dully in the warm firelight, serving as a jarring reminder of the danger that surrounded Josh on a daily basis. He didn't work undercover like Anthony had, but that didn't make his job as a homicide detective any less perilous.

Before she could question if having the pistol so readily accessible was necessary, he began closing her drapes, shutting out the darkness, the tempestuous weather, shrouding them in a different kind of foreboding.

Unease slithered down her spine. "Josh, what are you doing?"

"Closing the drapes." The smooth muscles across his back flexed as he gave the cord one last tug. The curtains fell into place, swaying gently.

"I prefer them open."

He moved away from the covered slider and toward her. "I don't like that I can't see out at night, and anyone who happens to walk by can see in."

"Anthony used to say the same thing. I believe I called him paranoid." The implication that Josh suffered the same affliction was clear.

She'd meant to lighten the moment, but her attempt fell flat.

Josh stopped a foot away, bringing with him a heat more intense than the fire in the hearth. His gaze locked with hers, shrewd and uncompromising. "Anthony must have had a lot to be paranoid about."

2

ANTHONY MUST HAVE HAD a lot to be paranoid about.

Apprehension crawled along Paige's skin. Josh's comment wasn't an off-the-cuff jest, or a typical response to her own remark about paranoia. There wasn't an ounce of humor in his too-serious expression or the grim set of his jaw.

It had been a statement of fact.

Paige lowered herself to the couch, recalling Anthony's behavior the last time he'd been home before his death, remembering how on edge he'd been. Every little sound that echoed in their house had made him so suspicious he hadn't been able to sleep at night. He'd closed the curtains in every room, latched the locks on all the doors and windows and prowled restlessly through the house. On their last morning together, she'd found him sleeping on the couch, sitting upright, his body finally claimed by exhaustion. His gun was clutched in his hand, resting in his lap, index finger curled around the trigger. When she'd gently touched his shoulder to wake him, he'd bolted off the couch and leveled his pistol straight at her heart. His eyes were wild, his savage expression that of the stranger he'd become.

She'd waited for the gun in her husband's hand to explode, wondering in that flash of an instant what kind of terror drove him to such extremes. Her body began to tremble, and the hot, aching tears she'd stored for months rushed forward.

Finally, he'd lowered the gun, looking around as if his surroundings were coming into focus. He hadn't apologized or comforted her for scaring the life out of her. Instead, his gaze had narrowed into a menacing glare and he'd roared, "Goddammit, Paige, don't *ever* sneak up on me that way again!"

What little was left of her feelings for him shattered in that moment. "It's over, Anthony," she'd told him, and meant it. "I can't keep living like this. I want the divorce I asked for months ago."

"No." It was the same answer he'd given her the first time she'd asked for a divorce. He didn't want her because he loved and cherished her. No, Anthony always had a compulsion to be in control, and that meant domineering her life, as well.

Without another word on the subject, he'd packed his duffel bag and was gone within the hour. By the end of the day she'd contacted a lawyer and begun divorce proceedings. A few days later, a dissolution of the marriage had no longer been necessary. Anthony had made her a widow.

Josh sat beside her on the couch, nearest to the gun on the end table, and took a drink of his black coffee. Then his gaze met hers. "Did Anthony tell you anything at all about the case he was working on?"

Looking away from those dark eyes that seemed to penetrate too deeply, she reached for her own coffee and took a sip of the sweetened brew. Instead of setting the cup back down, she kept her fingers wrapped around the warm ceramic mug. "He never discussed his cases with me, and I learned never to ask."

Whenever she'd expressed an interest in his work, he

would snap at her and use the excuse that his cases weren't up for discussion. It wasn't that she wanted to know details, she only sought to understand the appeal of Anthony's driving need to work on dangerous, undercover cases.

When Josh made no comment, she risked a glance at him, disturbed by the enmity touching his expression and the tense set of his shoulders. Carefully, she set her mug on the coffee table in front of her. "Josh, what's going on?"

He blew out a rough breath, set his coffee cup next to hers, and dragged his fingers though his still damp hair. He muttered a raw expletive, then said, "Anthony's death wasn't an accident."

She frowned. It took a few seconds for his meaning to sink in. When it did, her stomach churned. The alternative was too horrible to contemplate, yet she found herself choking out in a voice barely above a whisper, "You mean he was…murdered?"

Josh's gaze held a wealth of sympathy and compassion, but he didn't soften his reply. "Yes."

"Dear Lord," she breathed in horror. The finality of that one word rocked her world, made her mentally grope for answers to put this recent revelation into perspective. "But you told me nobody knew Anthony was an undercover officer."

"They didn't, Paige, I swear." He leaned forward, bracing his forearms on his hard thighs, his gaze holding hers. "According to the men still undercover on the case, the bad guys still don't know Anthony was a cop."

"I don't understand." Paige struggled to decipher what Josh was telling her, but her muddled mind refused to accept the truth. "If they didn't know Anthony was a plant, why would they kill him?"

He gave her question a moment's consideration. "I think you'd have a better understanding of the situation if I started from the beginning."

"Please do." She was beyond caring that she sounded haughty and demanding; she desperately wanted this awful turn of events to make some kind of sense.

Josh stood and went to the fireplace, a restless energy surrounding him. He tossed more logs on the grate and a burst of sparks filtered up the chimney. Taking the poker, he repositioned the wood, giving the chore more attention than it warranted.

"Josh, make me understand," she pleaded.

Rubbing at the rigid muscles at the base of his neck, he glanced over his shoulder at her. The deep frown creasing his brows gave her the distinct impression he wanted to be anywhere but here, briefing her on the facts surrounding Anthony's death.

"Anthony went undercover on this particular case to infiltrate a jewel-smuggling ring that has been trafficking rare and exotic gems into the Keys," he explained, his voice low and threaded with an odd reluctance. "Anthony's main objective was to get as close to the mob boss as possible. Our hope was that he'd be trusted enough to become a runner, someone they would involve in the actual smuggling. We needed that so we could bust the bad guys in the actual act of importing the jewels, which would give us enough evidence to prosecute."

Paige pushed her thick fall of hair away from her face with a slightly shaking hand. What Josh described was exactly the kind of classified work she imagined Anthony did, full of risk and a dangerous, deadly kind of thrill.

She had a sudden understanding of how ignorance could be bliss.

"The man heading the organization, Victor Carranza, was very elusive, and Anthony had a difficult time establishing a relationship with him." Josh jabbed the logs one last time before setting the brass poker back in its stand. Then he turned around and faced her. "There's a woman who works for Carranza. Her name is Bridget, and she's one of his runners. Since Anthony had little luck with Carranza himself, he switched tactics and decided to focus his attention on Bridget. It didn't take Anthony long to get close to her. Within a couple of weeks, Anthony knew most of Carranza's contacts."

He started toward her, his gaze troubled, yet bright with determination. Sitting on the cushion next to her, he gently grabbed her hand, holding it within his palm. Though his fingers were warm, a startling chill thinned her blood.

"Paige..." He cut himself off, a muscle in his lean jaw flexing. "Christ, there's no easy way to say this."

A peculiar combination of anticipation and unease tripped up her pulse. "Say what, Josh?"

Regret softened his features, and he stroked his fingers along her hand. The display of solace only served to unnerve her.

He let out a slow breath, his mouth thinning in displeasure. "From what we've learned, Anthony was having an affair with her—"

Snatching her hand from his grasp, she bolted off the couch and crossed the room. Standing by the fireplace, her back to Josh, she closed her eyes and wrapped her arms around her middle, doing her best to hold herself together. She hadn't bargained for the more sordid details of Anthony's undercover assignment, never would have guessed Josh would be the one to force her to deal with issues she'd deliberately tried to ignore.

So, Anthony *had* been having an affair. Josh's announcement shouldn't have surprised her, or hurt as much as it did. She'd had her suspicions before Anthony died. They hadn't made love in months, and he hadn't so much as kissed her or touched her beyond necessary contact. She'd chalked up his remoteness to stress on the job, until she'd discovered three foil packets in the inside pocket of his leather bomber jacket. What did he need condoms for when he'd insisted she go on the Pill? When she'd confronted him with the evidence, he'd laughed and told her the guys at the station must have played a joke on him and planted the prophylactics.

Knowing he'd deny any wrongdoing, she found it difficult to argue with his convenient excuse. Ultimately, she hadn't believed him.

Since his death, she had made more discoveries, and had found irrefutable evidence of his infidelity: credit-card purchases for women's lingerie, jewelry and other feminine frivolities she'd never received, charges for elegant hotel suites she'd never enjoyed with her husband, and expensive dinners at five-star restaurants she'd never been to.

Now one of the women he'd cavorted with had a name. The sense of betrayal twisting through her was excruciating.

The weight of Josh's hands came to rest on her shoulders, and she flinched at his touch. She'd been so lost in her own unsettling thoughts she hadn't realized he'd come up behind her.

"I'm so sorry, Paige," he said, his voice contrite, but fueled by an underlying purpose. "The woman Anthony was having an affair with—"

Abruptly, she jerked away, whirled around to face him, and held up a hand to waylay his words. "I don't want to hear this!"

He braced his hands on his hips and glowered at her, all previous signs of gentleness and understanding gone. The firelight painted his skin a warm gold hue, made his dark, silky hair gleam, giving him the appearance of a merciless, fierce warrior. "You don't have a choice." His tone was succinct and brooked no compromise.

"What Anthony did, and with whom, is now a moot point," she snapped, her emotions frayed. "He's *dead!*"

"What Anthony did was steal a valuable diamond-and-emerald necklace!" he shot back, his tone just as loud and angry.

She gasped in shock and reeled back. Denial came just as swiftly. "You're wrong!" Her voice cracked, right along with a chunk of her composure. She couldn't, wouldn't, believe what he was saying. "Goddammit, Josh, you're wrong!"

"I wish to hell I was, Paige." He stepped toward her, and when she backed up out of his reach, he swore. "Anthony stole the Ivanov necklace from a collection of jewels that was smuggled in from Russia. The diamonds and emeralds in that necklace are reportedly worth over a million dollars, and Anthony stole it from the woman he was having an affair with before she could hand the collection over to Carranza. They knew the piece was missing, but it took Carranza a few weeks to track down who'd taken it. All traces led back to Anthony."

Tears burned the back of her throat and stung her eyes. She choked on a sob she couldn't hold back. "You're lying!" Her accusation lacked conviction, but she wanted so badly for this moment in time to be nothing more than a nightmare, a trick of her imagination.

But Josh had never lied to her before.

"The investigation has been concluded and the facts confirmed by the men still working undercover on the case," Josh ruthlessly went on. "The woman set him up for that explosion in the boat. Carranza found out he'd taken the Ivanov necklace, and when he denied it, they killed him. They had no idea he was a cop—"

Unable to listen to any more, incapable of understanding her husband's multiple deceptions, she let out a deep, guttural cry that was ripped from the depths of her soul. "Nooo!" She came at Josh, fists flailing, striking out at him for every one of her husband's indiscretions, his betrayal, his disloyalty. "No, no, no!" All at once her blows landed on his chest, his arms, his shoulder. A crack resounded as her fist unexpectedly connected with his jaw.

"Dammit," he bit out, and caught her wrists, the strength of his grasp easily restraining her.

She stopped thrashing, tilted her head back and looked into Josh's eyes. They were filled with the same haunting emotions that gripped her. She realized that Anthony's actions had hurt him, too.

Oh, God, she felt so torn, disillusioned, and so painfully, horribly alone. Then the dam broke, the sheer magnitude of her anguish wracking her body with great soul-wrenching sobs.

Without a word, knowing what she needed, Josh

pulled her into his arms, cradled her against his chest and held her while she purged herself of all her pent-up grief and rage. He stroked her back, murmuring soothing words as her tears dampened his skin, but not once did he tell her everything was going to be all right.

"Why, Josh?" she whispered achingly, once the worst of her emotional barrage had ebbed. She lifted her head from his shoulder to look into his eyes, seeking more answers. "What did I do wrong?"

"Oh, sweetheart," Josh whispered, their faces so close she could feel the caress of his warm breath on her lips. Lifting his hand, he brushed his knuckles tenderly across her cheek, wiping away the last of the moisture lingering there. "It was nothing you did. It was just the way Anthony was."

She was beginning to understand that, but it didn't lessen the pain of his duplicity. "I never really knew him."

"I don't think any of us did," he admitted. Drawing in a steadying lungful of air that expanded his chest, he went on in a rush, "Paige, there's more I need to tell you."

Her stomach clenched, and before she could think about what she was doing, she pressed her fingers over his lips. "No, Josh," she said in a ragged voice. "Please, no." She wrapped her arms around his neck, not caring that she was clinging, because it felt so good to be held like this, as if she meant something to someone.

It had been so long.

"Ah, Paige..." A shudder rippled the length of him and she sensed that self-control of his slip; she could feel his acquiescence in the way his breathing deepened, the way his hands slowly, languidly slid down her spine and gripped her hips—not to push her away, but to bring her closer still.

The awareness they'd fought to suppress for years sizzled to life between them—a need so compelling it shook Paige to the very core.

Turning her head, she let her lashes drift shut and inhaled Josh's clean male scent. A deep, forgotten longing stole through her, and she boldly skimmed her lips along his jaw, tasting his skin, seeking a more elemental comfort, a more primal contact.

She needed this affirmation of her existence. She needed to feel alive, wanted and desired. Swallowing her pride, she told him in a soft, husky whisper, "I need you, Josh."

A rough groan rumbled in his chest and he touched his soft, warm mouth to hers. The gesture started out as a chaste kiss, tentative and searching, until she parted her lips under the coaxing heat of his own. Then, the tenor changed. So did all the rules they'd lived by for the past three years.

His tongue daringly breached barriers he'd never explored before, gliding deeply, erotically into uncharted territory to stake a claim. *His claim.* Her mouth was just as insatiable, opening wider to receive the seductive thrust of his tongue, to welcome the heat and unbridled hunger exploding between them. Her head spun, and she tingled with the wonderful sensation of being desired. Slipping her fingers into the silky hair at his nape, she arched sinuously against him.

A strong arm slid around her back, cradling her within his embrace, making her feel sheltered and protected. Her breasts were crushed against his chest, and her nipples tightened against the lacy webbing of her bra. His other hand roamed lower, beneath the hem of her sweater, to cup her bottom, nudging her intimately closer. The press of his erection between them sparked a thrill of arousal that pooled in her belly and between her thighs.

She moaned into his mouth. Need rose swiftly, overwhelming in its power, making the entire length of her body quiver. But the ache in her heart, the one she'd lived with for what felt like an eternity, was still too sharp, still too acute.

She wanted it to go away. Wanted to forget everything but the luxurious pleasure Josh's touch evoked. If only for this one night, she didn't want to think, she wanted to *feel.*

Josh dragged his mouth from Paige's and nuzzled the fragrant curve of her neck, found the silky hollow beneath her ear with his mouth.

For too long he'd imagined what it would be like to kiss Paige with unrestrained passion and have her respond with such eagerness and fire…fantasized in the darkest hours of the night about making love to her, possessing her heart, body and soul.

Now that temptation beckoned him. *She* beckoned him.

Lifting his head and loosening his hold, he stared into green eyes glittering with desire, and so much need. So much anguish. Those vulnerable emotions threatened his restraint, because he wanted to ease her pain any way he could. And right now, she wanted the tenderness of human touch to wipe away the ugliness.

His touch.

He was close to giving in. His honorable intentions wavered within him, playing tug-of-war with the reckless urge to do things to her, with her, he'd only dreamed about.

How could that be right? "Oh, God, Paige..."

"Josh, please," she begged in a sexy, throaty voice that wreaked havoc with his sanity. She dragged her tongue across her lush bottom lip, pink and swollen from his kiss.

The craziness of wanting her started all over again. When he opened his mouth to issue a protest, she cut him off.

"Don't say anything." Her beautiful gaze beseeched him in a way no words could. "I need you to make me forget. Just for tonight." Grasping the hem of her sweater, she pulled it over her head and dropped it on the floor, leaving her clad in a pretty bra that he could see right through, and leggings that molded to her hips and long legs. Her hair tumbled in tousled, sensual disarray around her shoulders.

Denying her became a distant thought. Loving her and giving her a safe haven for the night became his sole purpose. Holding her gaze, he reached out and slid his fingers from the pulse fluttering in her throat, down the slope of a perfectly curved breast cupped in sheer floral lace, across a taut nipple—and heard her breath catch in her throat—and continued to the front clasp of her bra. He hesitated, knowing with this one action, he was agreeing to her terms.

Just for tonight.

He'd never been one for one-night stands, and his feelings for Paige made what was about to happen even more complicated. But he couldn't walk away. Not when they needed each other so much.

With a flick of his thumb and index finger he unhooked her bra, watching as the sides separated to reveal pale mounds of flesh tipped with dark centers. His gut clenched, and he spontaneously buried both hands in her thick, luxurious hair and brought her mouth back to his.

He meant to go slow and savor every kiss, every sigh, every nuance of what made her so special, so sweet. He meant to wallow in her softness, her feminine scent, her response to his touch. He meant to show her just how much she meant to him, and take the time to worship her with his hands, his mouth, his sex.

Those good intentions fled the moment her lips parted beneath his and she sucked his tongue into her mouth. She was too needy to go at a leisurely pace, too out of control to tame. So he let her dictate how far she wanted to go, how wild and fast she wanted this ride to be.

The tempest of the rain and wind outside was nothing compared to the velocity gathering momentum between them. The frenzied way Paige's hands explored his chest, skimmed down the flat plane of his belly, then tugged impatiently on the drawstring of his sweatpants left Josh no time to think about getting her to a nice, soft bed. Where he took Paige didn't seem to matter to her. She was too caught up in her own private urgency to care. Her flattened palms smoothed into the waistband, loosening the drawstring, giving her more slack to glide her hands inside to seek warmer, harder flesh.

Knowing he was a goner if she so much as touched his straining erection, he abruptly pulled her with him to the plush carpeting. They ended up on their knees in front of the crackling fire, facing each other, their mouths still fused, tongues mating. He cupped her full breasts and caressed them with his hands, rolled her nipples between his fingers. She whimpered, and tugged at his sweatpants again.

He broke their kiss and grabbed at her groping

hands. "Not yet, sweetheart," he murmured, and pressed her down, until she was lying before him. Hooking his fingers into the waistband of her leggings, he swept them and her panties down her long legs, tossing the clothing aside.

And then he sat back and looked his fill, awed by her loveliness, and the trusting way she parted her thighs for him to slide in between. Firelight warmed her skin to a shimmery peach hue and spun gold in her hair and the thatch of curls covering her femininity. She was all supple curves, endlessly long limbs, and sexy as hell.

He'd wanted her for so long, and now she was his.

His gaze gradually climbed back up to her face, stopping to admire each attribute on the way. "You're absolutely beautiful," he told her, and guessed by the flush staining her cheeks that Anthony hadn't told her that often enough.

And because he didn't know what tomorrow would bring, and the days following, he set about showing her just how alluring he found her, how desirable, how delicious. He lavished every inch of her in kisses, starting at her instep, moving to the arousing spot behind her knee, and dragging his mouth along thighs that quaked in anticipation. His tongue dipped into her navel, laved her breasts, then he suckled her nipple deep into his mouth. With a strangled cry, she plowed her fingers through his hair and held him to her, her body moving insistently beneath his.

He didn't give in to her silent demands. He wasn't done with his exploration. Her sensitive neck was a delight he thoroughly enjoyed, her mouth a treasure trove of erotic pleasures he indulged in. He hadn't known French kisses could taste so damn good. With

her, they held the flavor of heaven, the essence of forever.

The sweet, delicate taste reminded him of the only
other place he hadn't sampled; he'd deliberately saved
the best for last. He sat up between her knees and shim-
mied the rest of the way out of his sweatpants. But instead of sliding over and into her, he took a more brazen approach he wasn't sure she'd approve of. She
didn't stop him when he used his palms and caressed
from her bent knee to her thighs and slowly guided her
legs further apart. Didn't object when he lowered his
mouth and nuzzled her, and drew deeply of her scent.
Didn't protest when he slicked his thumb over petal-
soft folds damp with her arousal. Didn't demur when
his tongue joined in the foray and stroked her intimately.

She closed her eyes on a sigh and entwined her fingers in his hair, shamelessly letting him have his way
with her. There were no barriers between them, no restrictions. The moan of complete surrender that purred
in her throat, her openness and the unconditional faith
she gave him humbled him like nothing in his life ever
had. Those elements also drove him on, made him ruthless in taking what he wanted.

It didn't take her long to find a shattering release, one
that made her cry out and tremble and push frantically
against his shoulders at the intensity of such an all-
consuming orgasm. He rode out the climax with her,
taking her all the way.

Only when she'd touched back down to earth did he
ease his body over hers, bracing his forearms on either
side of her head.

He caught a glimpse of fever-bright eyes before her

lashes drifted downward, concealing her emotions. His jaw hardened in resolve.

Gently grasping her face between his palms, he held her so she couldn't turn away, so she had no choice but to meet his gaze. "Look at me, Paige," he said, his tone slightly gruff. It wasn't a matter of her knowing who was about to make love to her—instinctively he knew he'd given her more in the last half hour than Anthony had in three years of marriage—but no way was he going to let her retreat into herself after what they'd just shared...and certainly not before what they were going to share.

Her eyes opened, and a myriad of emotions danced in the reflection of dying firelight. Most prominent was the deep, painful heartache he'd contributed to this evening, and an ocean of longing he believed he was a direct part of. There wasn't much he could do about the first emotion, but he could cater to the second.

Her hands slipped down the slope of his back, over his buttocks, rocking him closer, until the tip of his shaft penetrated ever-so-slightly.

She shuddered and arched. "Josh, come inside me," she said in a wispy voice.

The image her words incited were powerful enough to make him do just that. Literally. *Before* he had the luxury of sheathing himself within her. But he didn't want their time together to end so quickly, didn't want the night, this moment, to slip away anytime soon. So, he bent his head and kissed her. Slow and wet and rapacious, making her wild again, making him burn, building them both toward the completion of everything that had come before.

She was ready for him, and he couldn't wait a second longer.

She was so tight, so snug, that the first deep plunging thrust took them both by surprise. She gasped sharply as her body stretched to accommodate his size, his length. He groaned as her passage softened around him, accepted him, enveloped him until he couldn't tell where he ended and she began. She was as primed as a woman could be, yet there was a certain resistance that came from a long period of abstinence.

Then all thought fled as she began undulating her hips, making him slide deeper still, submersing him in silky heat. With a rough groan, he caught her heels and pulled her legs tight around his hips. The position offered him greater access, and he took advantage of it, giving her the wild ride she wanted.

She nipped at his jaw aggressively, then gently sank her teeth into his neck, only to soothe the bite with her tongue. He felt that slow, wet lap all the way to his groin. He grew harder, impossibly thicker. Tossing his head back, he pumped rhythmically, over and over, driving toward completion.

He felt the first tiny quiver of her release convulse around him, heard a sob break from her throat along with his name. He opened his eyes and looked down just in time to see the ecstasy and pleasure on her face as she came for him. That was all it took. His own climax slammed into him, powerful and unrelenting, until finally he buried his face in her neck and let out a long, spent groan.

He lay there on top of her, still inside her, awed by the indescribable feelings their lovemaking evoked. Never, with any of the women he'd ever slept with, had he ever experienced such fire and passion—or such a primal need to possess.

But then he'd never loved a woman the way he loved

Paige, and that made all the difference between sex and making love.

Wanting the precious, simple moment to last a little while longer before reality intruded, he pressed warm kisses on her neck. A shiver raced through her body, making her breasts swell beneath the crush of his chest.

He found himself smiling, and took great satisfaction in her automatic response. She stroked his hair, his relaxed shoulders, the firm slope of his back, keeping him close. Her legs remained entwined with his, giving him no indication she wanted him to leave her. His body quickened.

And then he felt something warm and wet seep against the hand still buried into her hair at the side of her face. Frowning, he lifted his head and stared into luminous green eyes filled with silent tears. She blinked and another single drop escaped.

His heart wrenched in his chest. He brushed the moisture away with his thumb, wondering at the source of those tears. "Paige?" he questioned.

A watery smile curved her mouth. "Don't ask me to explain what even I don't understand," she said, brushing her fingers along his jaw, right where she'd walloped him earlier. Her touch was soothing, but the look in her eyes was troubled. "Let's chalk it up to a very emotional night."

Her tears were a natural release after everything she'd been through that evening, he told himself, but he couldn't help but wonder, and worry, about the change to their relationship after what they'd just shared. They'd crossed boundaries and become lovers in a time of need. What would happen now? Would this be a one-night stand, or the beginning of something special for them?

Tomorrow would tell.

That simple thought led to another more complicated issue—the fact that he'd yet to tell Paige that Anthony's perfidy had put her life at risk.

Knowing her fragile emotional state couldn't withstand more shocking news, he decided the morning would be soon enough to discuss things. Moving off her, he stood. She sat up, too, reaching for her sweater.

He found her bout of modesty endearing, but unnecessary. "You don't need that, sweetheart. I've seen everything there is to see." Catching her hand before it closed around the article of clothing, he gave her an easy tug until she was standing before him in all her naked glory.

Letting out a breath that did nothing to ease the surge of heat heading straight to his groin, he glanced away and started toward the hall, pulling her along. "Come on, let's put you to bed."

She'd transformed the master bedroom from what had been a masculine domain into a feminine haven, her touch evident throughout. The furniture was frilly and Victorian, as was the four-poster bed. Lacy curtains framed the window, and the bedspread was made of mauve silk with matching ruffled pillows, which he tossed onto the brocade chair in the corner of the room. He pulled back the covers, waited until she slipped between the sheets, then adjusted the blanket around her shoulders.

"Get some rest, Paige," he said, and couldn't resist sliding his fingers through her silky hair one last time. "We'll talk in the morning."

He started back out of the room, but her husky voice halted him before he could retreat.

"Josh?"

He stopped and glanced back at her, though all he could see in the darkness was a huddled form beneath the covers. "Yeah?"

She hesitated, then, "Will you stay with me tonight and just hold me?"

It was the last thing he expected, and the last thing he'd refuse. "Let me take care of the fire, and I'll be back, okay?"

"Okay."

Less than five minutes later he returned, sliding into bed next to her. He snuggled up behind her, his muscular body pressing against soft womanly curves. Wrapping his arms securely around her waist, he cocooned their bodies in a warm, trusting intimacy. Long after Paige had fallen asleep, he savored the feel of her in his arms.

And realized he never wanted to let her go.

3

PAIGE OPENED HER EYES, blinked, then groaned and squinted at the slivers of sunshine filtering through the shutters covering her window. Stretching the kinks from her body, she rolled over to face the other side of the bed, expecting to find Josh sleeping beside her.

She was alone.

Raising herself on her forearm, she pushed her tangled hair from her face and glanced around the room, listening carefully for any signs of life beyond her closed bedroom door. The house was still and quiet, and everything outside was calm, making her wonder if the storm and Josh's visit last night had all been a dream. A dream that had begun with devastating news surrounding Anthony's death, and had ended with an incredibly erotic night of making love to Josh.

Still hovering between the lassitude of sleep and full wakefulness, she slid out of bed and headed to the bathroom, certain the whole episode had been some kind of bizarre illusion.

But it had seemed so real…

Switching on the light, she caught sight of her reflection in the large mirror over the dual-sink vanity. She was naked. That revelation was enough to cause a stirring of alarm, considering she never slept in the nude.

Bits and pieces flooded her mind, solidifying facts and wiping away any last remnants of slumber. Last night hadn't been a figment of her imagination. The proof mocked her—in the form of red patches on her skin caused by the light stubble that had been on Josh's jaw. She was marked everywhere! Branded by whisker burns!

She touched the abrasion on her neck; it was warm to the touch and a little sensitive. Her fingers fluttered lower, to the chafed skin on her breasts. Vivid memories leapt to life, of Josh rubbing his cheek gently against the plump flesh before flicking his tongue over her nipple. And then there were the pink scratches on her flat belly, and more evidence of whisker burn between her thighs. She lightly touched those scrapes, remembering how the raspy sensation had aroused her as much as his mouth and hands had, and recalling her shameless response to the wicked things he'd done to her.

A shudder rippled through her, and a low groan caught in her throat. She closed her eyes as much to shut out the arousing memories assaulting her senses, as to block out how rumpled and wanton she looked.

But she couldn't forget.

Another vision intruded, the image wispy and fleeting, like a dream. Only it hadn't been a dream, but reality in its purest sense. She'd slowly woken in the middle of the night, feeling lethargic but very aware of a large hand fondling her breasts and the press of an erection nestled against her bottom.

She recalled thinking she wanted him. Again. With the same desperation as the first time. But he'd gently eased her onto her belly, followed her with the length of his body, and whispered in her ear that this time they were going to take it slow and easy.

He'd made love to her lazily, their bodies so in sync,

it was hard to believe they'd been lovers for just one night. His lips pressed damp kisses on her neck, his tongue traced the shell of her ear. When he'd murmured so sexily, "Come for me," she'd unraveled and had done just that. He was with her all the way, taking them up that crest at a leisurely pace that drew out the pleasurable sensations shimmering between them.

Paige opened her eyes and stared at her horrified expression. She pressed her palms to her flushed cheeks. Oh, Lord, what had they done? What had *she* done? In a moment of weakness she'd sought comfort in Josh's arms, had bared herself emotionally and physically. His healing touch had been like a balm to her battered and bruised heart. He'd made love to her as if she were the only woman left on earth, had settled for no less than her full surrender.

In return, she'd given him her body, her heart, and the part of her soul that had been lost for so long. She'd always cared for Josh, possibly even loved him on some level beyond friendship. Last night had been a culmination of those feelings. She'd needed him as much as he'd needed her—needed to feel something other than the pain of Anthony's deception. Making love with Josh had wiped out the horrible truth about her husband for a few hours. With Josh, she'd felt more alive and desirable than she had in the past three years.

But it couldn't, and *wouldn't*, happen again. No matter what had transpired between them last night, no matter that Josh had claimed a part of her Anthony never had, involving herself with Josh beyond a platonic friendship was pure madness. Sheer stupidity. It had taken her three months to make difficult decisions about her future and decide what she wanted to do now that she had nothing substantial left to keep her tied to Miami. Especially when her entire family lived in Connecticut. The last thing she needed was her blossoming feelings for Josh to get in the way of her plans—plans she intended to expedite as a result of last night's encounter.

Ignoring the ache in her chest, she made a mental note to call her realtor and broker first thing Monday morning and begin the sale proceedings on the house and the Wild Rose. Then she rummaged a clip from the vanity drawer, secured her hair on top of her head, and stepped into the spacious tiled shower.

Fifteen minutes later she exited the bathroom, feeling more refreshed and awake, and determined not to allow the most emotionally fulfilling night of her life to interfere with her friendship with Josh.

She combed her hair and left it down, brushed her teeth, and put on a light application of makeup. Keeping in mind the various abrasions on her body, she opted for a hunter-green turtleneck and cream-colored slacks. Slipping on a pair of leather flats, she exited the bedroom, certain Josh was still there, considering she'd interrupted him before he could finish telling her about Anthony, and the case he'd been working on.

The living room was straightened, their coffee cups gone, the ashes in the grate completely cooled. The neat, folded pile of clothes and underthings she'd shed for Josh was the only evidence of what had transpired last night.

The sliding glass door leading to the deck was open, and through the screen she saw Josh leaning against the railing, staring out at the blue ocean, his long fingers wrapped around a coffee mug with curls of steam drifting from the rim. He was dressed in the clothes he'd worn yesterday, his shoulder holster back in place, his

Beretta tucked securely inside. His posture was deceptively relaxed, but she knew at any given moment those lean muscles of his could spring into action—in less than two seconds he could have his gun out of the holster and drawn. He was trained to protect and serve, and shoot to kill if the situation warranted it.

Then he turned, as if sensing she stood there, and she had no choice but to open the screen door and step out onto the deck. She had no intention of avoiding him, or their morning-after conversation. The sooner they hashed things out, the better.

But she hadn't counted on him looking at her with such tenderness. Never would have expected the sensual, possessive smile that curved his mouth. Couldn't have anticipated that his smoldering brown eyes would touch her as intimately as his hands and mouth had last night.

She damned her traitorous body for responding to him after her stern lecture to herself in the bathroom.

"Good morning," he said, bringing his coffee mug to his lips, watching her over the rim while he took a drink.

Even his voice was richer, she thought. Sexier than she could ever remember. It was a bad sign that she noticed. Real bad.

"Good morning," she replied easily. Coming up beside where he stood by the white wooden railing encasing the deck, she stared out at the expanse of sand stretching toward the beach, still damp from the previous night's rain. The bright sun shimmered off the calm ocean, and a cool breeze lifted her hair away from her face.

She filled her lungs with a breath of clean, sea air.

"Judging by the beautiful weather today, you'd never guess that there was such a ferocious storm last night."

"That's typical Miami weather for you."

"Yeah, I suppose it is." Like strangers, they were reduced to talking about the weather. Inane conversation when there were so many personal issues to address. She'd never had a problem talking to Josh before. Their ability to communicate freely was one of the things she'd loved best about their friendship. She hated to think that last night might have put a crimp in that aspect of their relationship.

An awkward silence stretched between them, until she wanted to scream in frustration. She could feel his gaze on her, knew he was watching her, and finally gathered the fortitude to look at him and be done with it.

Up close and personal, she noticed he looked different. Then the change registered—no dark stubble this morning. "You shaved," she said, the words escaping before she could stop them.

He ran a palm over his smooth cheek, a grin creasing his mouth. "Yeah. I used your razor. And your toothbrush. I hope you don't mind."

"Not at all." Considering the sensual things they'd done to one another during the course of the night, she wasn't about to balk at that simple intimacy.

Catching sight of a light, purplish-blue discoloration on his jaw, she felt a wave of remorse wash over her. Without thinking, she reached out and lightly touched the tender spot. "You're bruised." Her voice was as soft as her gently probing fingers.

Awareness stirred in the depth of his gaze, darkening with the warmth of desire. For her. "You've got quite a left hook."

Her pulse quickened, a feminine warning she heeded. Abruptly, she pulled her hand back. Lord, she couldn't even touch him anymore, not even in casual concern, without sparks igniting between them. "I'm sorry."

"Don't apologize for touching me," he said, deliberately misconstruing her apology. "I like the way your hands feel on me."

His blatant admission caused a frisson of heat within her. The rogue wasn't going to make this easy on her. "Josh, about last night—"

"Do you regret what happened?" he interrupted.

"No, I don't." She couldn't lie. She'd needed him in ways she couldn't explain. A part of her still did, but she didn't take the time to analyze those feelings. "But it happened for all the wrong reasons."

He set his empty coffee mug on the round glass table then pinned her with a direct look. "I'd like to think it happened for a few *right* reasons."

Like the need they had for each other. She pushed that thought aside and focused on the future, which didn't include giving her heart to another man who risked his life on a daily basis. "Josh, please don't do this."

"Don't do what?" Determination and an edge of anger flared in his eyes, turning them a rich shade of gold. "There's nothing to be ashamed of, or feel guilty about. We're both consenting adults, and we didn't hurt anyone by making love."

His approach was about as subtle as a battering ram. "No, I won't argue with that."

Her ambiguous agreement seemed to annoy him even more, as if he'd been expecting, wanted even, a debate. His mouth stretched into a tight line and his brows creased. "Are you on any kind of birth control?"

"Birth control?" she echoed, momentarily startled by his very personal question.

"Yeah, birth control." His hands came to rest on his lean hips, and his gaze locked on hers. "We didn't use any protection last night, Paige."

Her stomach took a dive, and she pressed a hand to her belly before she could consider what she was doing, and how her actions might look to Josh. "Uh, no, I'm not on any kind of birth control." She'd gone off the Pill when Anthony had died. The possibility of getting pregnant had been the furthest thing from her mind when she'd asked Josh to make love to her. "But I should be fine. My period is due to start soon."

Her verbal reassurance didn't alleviate the concern glinting in his eyes. "Will you let me know if you're pregnant?"

The image of herself round with Josh's child flashed in her mind, and her heart skipped a beat. She wanted children so very badly, had always dreamed of having a large family one day. But the emotional complication of having *Josh's* baby wasn't something she wanted to contemplate. Being pregnant would irrevocably change her life, force her to make choices and decisions she hadn't figured into the equation of her immediate future.

So she opted for more positive thoughts on the matter. "I'll let you know when I start my period." Desperately wanting a diversion from that intimate topic, she broached a more unpleasant issue she knew Josh would eventually address even if she didn't. "Last night you said there was more I needed to know about Anthony and the case he was working on."

It was his turn to shift mental gears. Grim resolve gradually replaced the firm possessiveness that had tightened his features. "Yeah, there's more."

She brushed back strands of hair fluttering across her cheek from the cool breeze. "I'm not going to like what I hear, am I?"

Slowly, he shook his head. "Probably not."

She appreciated his honesty as much as she dreaded what lay ahead. "Then just give it to me straight. No beating around the bush and no sugarcoating."

"Okay," he said very carefully, giving her the impression he was preparing her for the worst. "Your life is at risk."

She frowned, certain she'd misunderstood him. "Excuse me?"

"I said, your life is at risk." His words were succinct, leaving no doubt in her mind that she'd heard him correctly the first time. "Since Anthony denied having the Ivanov necklace I told you about, and apparently he didn't have it on him when he was killed, we've been informed by the other undercover officers that Carranza suspects you have the necklace or might know of its whereabouts."

"That's ludicrous!" Her voice was loud enough to send a nearby flock of seagulls into flight, their indignant squawks echoing along the shore. "I don't know where the necklace is!"

"I believe you, but Carranza may not." He stepped toward her and gently placed his hands on her shoulders. "They've searched all of Anthony's personal belongings and turned up nothing. It's only logical that Carranza would have you checked out next."

"Of course." Acid burned in her empty stomach, and

she swallowed to keep it from rising into her throat. "This Carranza person knew Anthony was married?"

"It wasn't a secret that Anthony was married. Carranza could learn that information easily enough. Since Anthony was having an affair, word spread that you were just a pampered wife and that you and Anthony pretty much lived your own private lives."

The bitterness finally escaped her in the form of broken laughter. It hurt, dammit, to think what a farce her marriage to Anthony had always been. To realize that Josh's words held so much truth.

She moved away, and he let her go. Realizing just how wobbly her legs were, she slid into a chair next to the table. Letting out a deep breath, she looked to Josh for guidance. "Now what am I supposed to do?"

"Right now, our undercover officers are reportedly having you checked out." Leaning his hip against the railing, he crossed his arms over his wide chest, looking every inch the tough, uncompromising detective he was. "As soon as they find some kind of evidence that you know something about the Ivanov necklace or its whereabouts, they're to let Carranza know."

"I told you," she said through gritted teeth. "I don't know anything about that necklace!"

Her snappish tone didn't faze him. "I know you don't, but the department has a strategy in mind, and it would be to our advantage to find the necklace. And we need your full cooperation to make the setup work."

She gave him a tight, angry smile. "Do I have a choice in the matter?"

"Not since you've become Carranza's main target. Lieutenant Reynolds and I agree that you need around-the-clock protection, but we can't risk planting a bunch of men around the house, or being obvious in our surveillance."

The ominous scenario his words projected caused a shiver of apprehension to skip down her spine. "The house has a security system." Remembering that she hadn't been using it when she'd opened the door to Josh last night, she added, "I'll make sure I have the alarm on whenever I'm home."

"That won't protect you once you leave the house. And we don't know where, when, or how Carranza will approach you."

Her skin crawled at the thought of this stranger, or any of his men, stalking her for something she didn't even have. "So what are you suggesting?"

He settled into the chair next to hers and braced his forearms on his knees. *Guarded* was the only term that could describe his expression. "Word is being spread that Anthony's widow has a live-in lover."

She gaped in disbelief. "What?" This ridiculous plan was going too far!

"Paige," he said, his patient tone cajoling her to be reasonable. "It's the only believable way for me to stay here and protect you until we bust Carranza."

Her mind registered the word *me*, as in *Josh*. Shock gave way to incredulity. "*You're* posing as my lover?"

"Yes." There was nothing in his serious expression to indicate that posing as her lover would be anything more than a job to him. A way to protect her, as he'd stated, despite that they *had been* lovers. "The undercover officers on this case have already filtered information about me to Carranza, which includes a false last name of Bennett, which you need to remember. Right now, I'm unemployed and living with you."

Her mind reeled with all the information he was

loading onto her, and she fought to deny it. "This is crazy!"

"It'll only be for a few weeks. A month, tops." He reached for her hand and tucked it between both of his, making her realize how cold and clammy her palm was next to his warm, dry one. "I'll do whatever it takes to protect you. So you can expect that I'll be by your side whenever possible."

"Even at work?" Surely he wasn't going to shadow her steps every hour of the day?

"Your life will resume as normal—"

"You call this normal?" she asked, unable to tamp down the horrible hysteria clawing its way to the surface. "Go to hell, Josh!" Standing, she jerked her hand out of his grasp and started for the deck stairs leading to the beach.

He was lithe and agile, moving out of his own chair and blocking her path before she could bolt. "I call this saving your life," he said, his tone low and ruthless enough to make her realize there would be no escaping him, or this awful situation, until it was officially over. "We'll be planting an undercover officer at your boutique, so you'll be protected while you're working. You'll never be alone, Paige, even when you think you are. There will always be someone watching over you, and for the most part, that will be me."

Her chin lifted defiantly. "And what if I tell you I don't want any part of this operation? That I refuse to cooperate?"

Something harsh and dangerous glittered in his eyes. "Then you could end up just like Anthony."

If there had been anything in her stomach at the moment, she was certain it would have ended up on Josh's loafers. Her entire body flashed hot, then cold. Little black dots danced in front of her eyes, and her vision began to blur. She knew she was going to faint, and she also knew there was nothing she could do about it.

Her knees buckled, and she heard a distant curse, then felt two hands wrap around her arms and guide her back until her knees hit something solid and she collapsed into a chair. A large hand cupped her neck and pushed her head down until it was between her knees.

"Breathe, Paige," he commanded.

She did, drawing much-needed oxygen into her lungs until the wave of dizziness and nausea passed. When she finally felt stable again, she lifted her head and found Josh kneeling in front of her.

Swallowing to ease the dryness in her throat, she managed a smile. "I did say no sugarcoating, didn't I?"

He laughed, the sound rough. "Yeah, you did." With a tenderness that made her heart catch, he smoothed her hair away from her face, then dragged his thumb along her cheek. "Sweetheart, I'm sorry Anthony left you in this mess. But it's too late to back out now, not with Carranza determined to find that necklace. It's essential to the case, and your own life, that the department has your full cooperation. That *I* have your full cooperation. You understand that, don't you?"

She understood that she'd be living with Josh for weeks and doing her best to avoid him and the memories of their one night together. She understood that her husband had been a criminal, even while he'd sworn to uphold the law. She understood that she'd have no life of her own until all this ended.

She hated every bit of it, but she understood.

"You have my full cooperation," she said in a whisper, and knew she'd live by that pledge. Because if she didn't, if she backed out and refused to participate in their grand scheme, she'd not only put her own life in jeopardy, but she'd risk Josh's life, and the lives of a dozen other men as well. Good, *honorable* men.

Now that she'd guaranteed her assistance, she wanted it over as quickly as possible. "So, what do we do now?"

He breathed an audible sigh of relief. "Now we find the Ivanov necklace."

THEY AGREED to start their search in the office, then work their way toward the front of the house. While Paige rummaged through drawers and closets for any shred of evidence, Josh checked the more inconspicuous spots in the rooms, odd places where Anthony could have rigged a false drawer, or used furniture as a prop to conceal the million-dollar necklace.

Nothing was left unexplored. No square inch of any room left untouched. Their search was thorough and lengthy—and companionable. The earlier personal strain between them had ebbed in view of the more pressing matter at hand. However, Josh had no intention of letting Paige conveniently dismiss what had happened the night before. Had no intention of letting her forget how simple need had evolved into desire and passion.

Last night had changed so much between them. Paige needed time to sort out her feelings, to come to terms with the changes in their relationship. Josh understood that, especially after everything he'd heaped on her in the past eighteen hours.

Right now, they had a necklace to find. Later, he'd concentrate on them.

"So, Detective Marchiano, what's the great plan if we find the necklace?"

Josh replaced a watercolor painting back on the wall, then turned and gave her a wry grin. They were in her bedroom, and three hours into the search. She stood just outside of the master bathroom, having just gone through the drawers and cupboards beneath the vanity.

"Your faith in finding the Ivanov necklace astounds me." He moved to the bed—determinedly blocking out images of Paige so warm and willing beneath him on that mattress—and patted down the throw pillows for any foreign lumps. "Concentrate on *when*, not *if*."

Paige stood, hands on her hips, her gaze scanning the room, scrutinizing everything with a critical eye. "I told you that I've gone through most of Anthony's things, and I haven't found anything that would indicate he had a million-dollar necklace in his possession." Moving to the nightstand, she opened the top drawer and sorted through the contents. "I haven't come across a receipt for a safety-deposit box, or anything else of that nature."

"I don't think he'd use a safety-deposit box for this." He stripped the covers off the bed and began inspecting the mattress for any odd seams or pockets. "I don't know that for sure, of course, but if I'd stolen the necklace I'd hide it in a way that isn't traceable by some kind of paper trail."

She glanced over her shoulder at him as he picked up the ceramic lamp on the nightstand and checked to make sure it hadn't been tampered with in any way. "If there is no evidence of the necklace and its whereabouts, then how does this Carranza person know that Anthony stole it at all?"

He noted her concerned expression before heading

toward the armoire against the far wall. "Good question," he acknowledged, silently admiring the way she addressed important facts most people wouldn't even consider. She was thinking like a detective, though he suspected she wouldn't appreciate being enlightened as to her natural investigative instincts.

"From what we've learned, Anthony made the mistake of contacting a guy who fences stolen merchandise and asked him if he was interested in some diamonds and emeralds." Opening the double doors to the armoire, he pulled out a cedar-lined drawer and found his hands immersed in a froth of silk and lace lingerie.

Damn. Heat licked through his veins, spiraling low. Quickly and efficiently he sifted through the sexy stuff that smelled as feminine as Paige. He found too much that piqued his interest, and nothing to warrant an extensive investigation of the contents of this particular drawer. He slammed it shut. Unfortunately, there was nothing he could do to banish the erotic images of Paige wearing a pair of those sheer panties and a matching wispy camisole.

"So, what happened?" Paige asked, jarring him out of his fantasy and effectively dousing his arousing mental vision.

He glanced over his shoulder. She slipped a hardbound book back into the nightstand and looked up at him with wide eyes full of interest. "Apparently, the fence has done business with Bridget before, and had heard about the missing Ivanov necklace. He knew he'd be rewarded for finding the jewels, not to mention stay on Carranza's good side, and tipped Bridget off about Anthony's inquiry."

She raised a brow and stood. "Since there was no

hard evidence that Anthony actually had the necklace, that's pure speculation, don't you think?"

He liked the way her mind worked, the way she didn't settle for a pat explanation. "Yes and no," he admitted. He took a moment to move the armoire and check the carpeting beneath, then arranged it back into place. "Bridget confronted Anthony about the inquiry, and he admitted he had the necklace and told her he'd cut her in on the deal. She's very loyal to Carranza and didn't go for it. When Carranza challenged him, Anthony denied everything. Carranza isn't known for leniency or second chances."

"No, it doesn't seem so, does it?" She rubbed her arms through the sleeves of her turtleneck, as if experiencing a sudden chill, though the room was comfortably warm. "So what are we going to do when we find the necklace? Give it back to Carranza?"

"Hell, no." She might be smart with investigative theories, but she was more than a little naive when it came to street intelligence. The vulnerability brought out his protective instincts, made him choose his explanation carefully. "We need the necklace as a lure. Carranza wants the Ivanov necklace, and we want him. This time, we're going to nail him."

She frowned. "How?"

He removed another picture from the wall, found nothing out of the ordinary, and replaced it. "Remember that portrait you had taken for Anthony on your first anniversary? You know, the one where you're wrapped in that white fur?"

His question surprised her, and her answer came hesitantly. "Yes, I remember."

And there was no way he could ever forget it. When Anthony had shown him a wallet-sized replica of that

16 x 20 portrait, Josh had been stunned by the transformation in Paige. Gone was the beautiful, conservative woman, and in her place was a seductive vixen. It had been one of those sexy, sensual portraits, soft and unfocused, like something straight out of a man's fondest fantasy. She'd been posed on her side, with a white fur wrap draped strategically along her sleek curves. One hand held the fur to her breasts, displaying a hint of cleavage and leaving her shoulders bare. One long leg slipped out of the folds so it appeared she wore nothing at all beneath the fur covering. Her thick, dark hair was tousled enticingly around her face, and she was looking into the camera with a provocative smile that promised endless pleasures.

Yeah, the portrait was perfect for what he had in mind. "Where is it?"

"I packed it away."

"You need to unpack it."

Judging by the wariness turning her eyes a deep shade of green, she wasn't too thrilled with the direction of their conversation. "Why?"

"The department has commissioned an artist to paint your portrait and add the Ivanov necklace. That picture would be perfect to use."

"I'd hardly think so," she argued. "Josh, the only thing I'm wearing in that picture is a white fur wrap!"

"Which will offset the necklace beautifully," he reasoned. "Once the portrait is done, which should take about a week, we'll hang it in your office at the Wild Rose."

Her jaw literally fell open, and she looked at him as if he were a few rounds short of a full clip. "Why in the world would I hang a portrait of myself? And one that's so..."

"Sexy?" he offered.

"Yes!"

She looked so indignant, he couldn't stop the grin tugging the corner of his mouth. "Because that's the kind of woman you've been portrayed as, someone who's pampered and a little pretentious. And you are sexy, Paige," he said. Then he added in a soft, meaningful tone, "Besides, you would have to hang a portrait that was a gift from your lover, wouldn't you?"

She fingered the high collar of her turtleneck, where a becoming shade of pink was slowly rising. "Don't you think this is taking things too far?"

"Nope." He headed toward the walk-in closet, the last place they needed to search. She followed at a discreet distance. "Once the picture is up, our plant will tell Carranza that he's heard about the portrait in which you're wearing the necklace. That's all it will take for Carranza to pay you a visit."

"And put a gun to my head and demand the necklace?" she asked sarcastically from behind him.

He immediately tossed out the horrible image her question projected in his mind. It wasn't a scenario he wanted to consider at the moment, though there would be precautions taken to avoid such a situation.

Turning on the light in the closet, he began sliding the clothes on hangers aside so he could check the wall behind. "Our sources tell us he's not into violence unless absolutely necessary. Our guess is that he'll make a few inquiries about the necklace and find out what you know about it. He might even pretend interest in purchasing it."

She stretched and retrieved a blue-and-gray striped box on the shelf above the hanging garments. "And what do I tell him?"

"You tell him that it was a gift from your husband, and play it like it's nothing more than costume jewelry."

"And what if he wants to buy it?" she countered.

"Then you tell him it's not for sale."

"Isn't that defeating the purpose of luring him?"

"No. He'll pursue his interest in the necklace," he said, confident of that. Turning, he found himself so close to Paige all he had to do was take half a step, lower his head, and he'd be able to kiss her like he'd been wanting to all day. Except he knew he'd never be able to stop at just one taste, and he knew she wasn't ready to accept the full brunt of his feelings for her. At least not in the light of day.

With a harsh sigh, he dropped to his knees on the floor, examining the molding around the base and checking the wall for any cutouts. "Our main goal is to get on Carranza's turf, which shouldn't be too difficult. He'll want to confiscate the necklace on his territory, surrounded and protected by his own people. It's what we want, too, since we have our own plants who can arrest Carranza when everything goes down."

"You make it sound so simple."

He glanced up, meeting her gaze, seeing her need for a reassurance he had no right to give. "No, it's not simple, Paige," he said honestly. "It's dangerous and it's risky, but I'll guarantee that you'll be protected in every way possible. I won't let anything happen to you."

Irritation flashed across her features and stretched her mouth into a grim line. "You can't make those kind of promises, so don't." She turned her back to him and proceeded to search through the drawers built into the closet.

In frustration, he blew out a stream of breath, hating

the tension vibrating between them. She was right, he couldn't make promises of immortality. He didn't have that kind of direct link to the big man upstairs. In truth, he had no way of predicting which way the chips would fall, and a part of him acknowledged that, with Paige's life at stake, he was nervous as hell about the outcome of this sting. He could only speculate how Carranza would react to the situation, could only hope his sources knew Carranza as well as they believed. It was like engaging in an intricate chess game with a master player, trying to think ahead and outsmart your opponent before making the slightest move.

And in order to think straight enough to counter any move Carranza or his men made, he had to keep his feelings for Paige, and his worry for her, secondary to his survival instincts.

As he put that important thought foremost in his mind, his fingers brushed over the frayed ends of the carpet. He frowned, then followed the ragged edge along the molding to the corner of the closet. The carpet wasn't tacked down as it should have been. Too easily, he stripped the piece back and found himself staring at a flat metal lid flush with the concrete foundation.

"I'll be damned," he muttered.

Paige knelt beside him. "What is it?" Her voice was as excited and eager as he felt.

Inserting his finger into the thumb-hole, he lifted the metal lid, revealing exactly what he'd anticipated. He looked at Paige and grinned triumphantly. "It's a built-in safe."

4

AFTER DISCOVERING the hidden safe, Josh immediately contacted his lieutenant, who sent out a pair of detectives to Paige's house, along with a team of forensic specialists to open the safe and secure the contents.

Two hours later, the extent of Anthony's corruption lay spread before them on the master-bedroom floor. The contents of the safe included over a hundred thousand dollars in cash, several kilos of cocaine, and other narcotic paraphernalia Josh highly suspected had been pilfered from various drug busts. Stashed in a canvas drawstring bag amongst the other evidence they'd seized, they found the stolen diamond-and-emerald necklace, directly implicating Anthony—and explaining how he'd been able to afford such a luxurious house, and a life-style that stretched beyond a cop's salary.

The proof of Anthony's illegal behavior burned in Josh's gut like acid. Judging by Paige's pale complexion and the shock etched on her features as she stared at the evidence, Josh knew she was just as appalled that she'd been so blindly deceived by the man she'd married.

She lifted her gaze, meeting his. The depths of her eyes were a dark, turbulent shade of green. "I had no idea, Josh," she whispered, her voice filled with confusion, and a deeper level of betrayal he fully understood. "How could I have not known?"

She wanted answers he wasn't comfortable expressing with half a dozen law-enforcement officials privy to their conversation. His view of the situation was pure speculation, and he had no desire to have his opinion thrown into the investigation.

Gently taking her arm, he guided her to the bedroom door and away from the men photographing the area and dusting the contents of the safe for fingerprints. "Why don't you go wait in the living room while these guys do their job, and I'll be there in a few minutes, okay?"

She stiffened at his order, but didn't argue. After one last troubled glance at the evidence, she headed down the hall and disappeared from Josh's sight. He shoved his fingers through his hair in frustration, torn between the desire to follow her and offer the emotional support she so obviously needed, and the duty his job required. He knew, though, that by aiding in the case work, he was helping Paige in a significant way—helping to save her life.

He came up beside Peterson, who was photographing the scene and each individual item confiscated from the safe. "I need a picture of the Ivanov necklace sent to Lieutenant Reynolds ASAP."

The older man with short-cropped salt-and-pepper hair nodded at Josh. "He'll have a complete set on his desk by tomorrow morning."

"Great." After escorting Paige to the Wild Rose in the morning, Josh planned to deliver the portrait he'd requested from Paige, along with a photograph of the necklace, so the artist they'd commissioned could get started on the painting.

Leaving the rest of the logging and reporting to the detectives working on the case, Josh went to find Paige.

She wasn't in the living room where he'd asked her to wait, which sparked a bit of annoyance that she'd blatantly ignored his request. Instead, he found her standing out on the beach a good hundred yards from the house, alone and vulnerable, making an excellent target for anyone who might be watching her.

Moving onto the deck, he slipped off his loafers and socks, and put them beside Paige's leather flats next to the wide set of wooden stairs leading to an endless playground of white sand. He headed toward where she stood just a few feet beyond the reach of the teasing and retreating surf.

She tilted her face toward the breeze. The position afforded him a glimpse of her profile—finely etched features that lent her a classical beauty. That wholesome, natural loveliness, combined with her impossibly sweet and generous nature, drew him like no other woman ever had.

After last night, the need to make her completely his was fierce and instinctive, a deep, primitive desire that skittered on the edge of recklessness. For three years, despite the unspoken awareness between them, they'd respected the perimeters of her marriage vows, even if Anthony hadn't. Josh was a man who strongly believed in commitment and the bonds of marriage, and would never have crossed those matrimonial boundaries.

Circumstances had changed. For both of them. Paige no longer belonged to a man who'd treated her as a possession, and there were no sacred vows or a friendship for Josh to betray.

Circumstances, as awful and devastating as they were, had brought them together, heightening emotions and desires they'd suppressed for too long. If Paige had her way, judging by the brief discussion they'd had that morning, he suspected she'd let last night become a distant memory. For him, forgetting wasn't even a remote possibility, not after discovering the sweet, honeyed taste of her, the soft feel of her body pressed beneath his, the intimate sounds she made when he eased deep inside her....

Having her just for one night would never be enough. Even now, his body quickened with the recollection of how incredibly responsive she'd been to his touch, how hungry she'd been...how *needy*. He'd been just as greedy, if not more so, because he wanted more than just one night of pleasure—he wanted endless tomorrows, and a lifetime of giving her everything she'd been missing in her marriage to Anthony.

He had a job to do and would protect her with his life. But he wasn't about to let her forget that he'd filled an emotional and physical void, wasn't about to let her tuck the memory away and revert to simple friendship. He'd give her time to adjust to the change—she deserved at least that much—but in the meantime he refused to pretend that nothing had happened between them.

She didn't hear him approach; he deliberately moved stealthily, determined to make her realize the kind of danger that would surround her. Moving up behind her, he grabbed her upper arm, wringing a startled gasp from her throat. She automatically jerked away and stumbled sideways, but his tenacious hold prevented her from landing on her bottom in the sand.

When she finally found her footing, she turned to face him. She didn't appear grateful for his assistance, not when he was responsible for shaking her up. Instead, she glared, her eyes shooting bright green flames of anger.

"Dammit, Josh," she hissed furiously, ineffectively tugging her arm from his grasp. "You could have warned me you were coming up behind me!"

He offered no leniency, nor did he let go of her. "Carranza or his men wouldn't have given a warning." His tone was as grim as the picture his words painted.

She hesitated for a moment, his meaning sinking past her indignant tirade. Then, she lifted her chin defiantly. "I'd appreciate it if you didn't sneak up on me that way."

If he hadn't been so intent on proving a point, he would have found her stubbornness amusing. But the situation was dire, her cooperation a necessity. "And I'd appreciate it if, in the future, you'd listen to my orders. I asked you to wait for me in the living room."

She glanced back at the house, her mouth thinning in disdain. "If you don't mind, I'd rather not be in the house right now."

He understood her aversion to the corruption filling her home, but she still needed to take precautions. "Fine. Next time tell me and either I, or another undercover officer, will escort you outside."

She crossed her arms over her chest, her expression reflecting her displeasure. "I resent this situation, Josh," she snapped.

He sighed wearily, and gave her a halfhearted smile. "No more than I do." Both of them had been betrayed by a man they'd trusted, and that knowledge cut deeply. More gently, he suggested, "Come on, let's go for a walk."

They strolled along the beach, near the water's edge where the wet sand made the going easier. Their walk was calming, peaceful, and just what they needed to release the stress of the past few hours.

"I'm having a hard time understanding what compelled Anthony to steal all that stuff," Paige commented, the first to break the companionable silence that had settled between them. "I feel so violated and deceived, in so many ways."

The pain and disillusionment lacing her voice grabbed at him, made him furious at himself because he'd been just as blind to Anthony's traitorous activities. "I think I know how you feel."

"Do you?" Her sharp, angry question was a search for answers. "How could I have lived with Anthony for three years, and never have known that I was married to a criminal?"

He glanced at Paige, resisting the urge to reach out and smooth away the frown lines between her brows. Touching her was becoming an obsession, and that was dangerous to his concentration. "Because you accept people at face value."

A mirthless little laugh caught in her throat and carried on the breeze. "Yeah, well, the joke's on me, isn't it?"

"On all of us, actually." He pushed the tips of his fingers into the front pocket of his jeans, keeping his stride along the beach as casual as Paige's. "Nobody wants to think that a cop might be on the wrong side of the law."

"So why did he do it?" she asked softly.

The answer to that question wasn't as simple as he would have liked. Glancing out at the ocean, he thought about all the possible replies that came to mind—the same ones he'd been mulling over for the past three months—and grasped the most logical explanation. "How much do you know of Anthony's past?"

She thought for a moment, then shrugged. "I know he's an only child and both his parents are dead. Other than that, Anthony refused to talk about his past. And after a while, I stopped asking." She gave him an odd look tinged with a deeper layer of suspicion. "Why? What does his past have to do with all this?"

Maybe nothing. Maybe everything. He tried to define his thoughts so they made sense to her. "You know I've known Anthony since we went through the Academy together."

She nodded, her gaze avid and curious. "Yes."

"When I met him, he was barely making ends meet. We became friends, and since he was living out of his VW Bug, I let him stay at my condo until he could afford a place of his own."

Back then, Anthony had been unpretentious enough to appreciate the simplicity of having a roof over his head. Somewhere along the way he'd changed. "One night after a few beers, he started talking about how he was going to be rich one day because he hated being poor. He'd grown up in a low-income neighborhood and struggled to keep himself and his mother from starving or being evicted from their tiny apartment. From what he told me, he didn't have an easy childhood."

"I never knew. He refused to talk about his past." She quietly digested what he'd told her, then asked, "Where was his father?"

"According to Anthony, his father left before he was born, and he lost his mother to pneumonia just before his eighteenth birthday. From there, he worked odd jobs, then joined the Academy, which is where I met him. I don't know his initial reasons for joining the Academy, but it was apparent from the beginning that he loved the danger and excitement of the job."

He rubbed at the back of his neck before continuing.

"About a year after we were on the force, Anthony started buying things he really couldn't afford. When I questioned him, he'd never give me a straight answer. I really didn't think his finances were any of my business, and just assumed he'd established a hell of a whole lot of credit. This went on for years, and when he didn't declare bankruptcy, I thought maybe he'd made some good investments that had paid off, but I never knew for sure." He slanted her a curious look. "Didn't you ever wonder how he was able to afford that prime piece of real estate you live in? The boat, the cars?"

"Yes, I wondered." They came across a cluster of smooth rocks, and Paige strolled in that direction. "When I asked about the purchases, he'd tell me he got a bonus or some other excuse I couldn't argue with. Anthony was adamant about taking care of the bills, so I never really had a good handle on our finances. And I had my own trust fund that my grandmother left me, so I bought whatever I wanted, when I needed it. That's how I was able to afford the Wild Rose."

He smiled, a slight curving of his mouth. "I remember." He also recalled how furious Anthony had been that Paige had openly defied him and bought the boutique—he'd had no control over her decision since she'd used her own money, and that fact rankled. Their marriage had seemed strained before that incident, but had gotten progressively worse after she'd opened the boutique and devoted her time and effort there. Anthony hadn't liked his wife working, yet he'd never given Paige any incentive to stay home.

But that was a different issue altogether, one that didn't belong in their current conversation. Paige sat down on one of the rocks and gazed out at the blue stretch of ocean. He opted to stand.

"I don't claim to be a psychiatrist, Paige," he said, bringing her attention back to him. "But taking Anthony's behavior into consideration, I'm guessing that his desolate childhood drove him toward greed. Money seemed to give him a warped sense of power and control, and judging by what we've discovered since his death, the need for prominence and wealth totally consumed his life." He shrugged, wishing he knew the truth about what had driven Anthony to take the outrageous risks he had—risks that had destroyed his life and put his wife's in jeopardy. "That's my theory, but we'll never know for sure."

"It certainly makes sense to me." Bitterness crept into her tone. "It didn't take me long to learn that Anthony thought of no one but himself."

Giving into the urge to touch her, he reached out and stroked her soft cheek, wanting to kiss her and make up for everything she'd lacked in her marriage to Anthony. Comfort. Understanding. Love. But she was still uncertain and wary, and he respected that even if he didn't like it. "I'm sorry you had to go through that."

"Yeah, me too." Her voice was sad, and she gently pulled his hand away from her face, as if his caress stirred too many memories of last night and how much she'd liked him stroking her skin. Touching her certainly brought to mind vivid, sensual images for him.

She drew a deep breath and released it slowly, as if mentally distancing herself from him. "Like my dad always used to say, 'You live, you learn, and move on a wiser person.'" She smiled, forcing a cheerful attitude that didn't quite reach her eyes. "That's exactly what I intend to do."

ONCE THE HOUSE was cleared of evidence and officials, Paige accompanied Josh to his condo to pick up clothes and personal items for him to keep at her place. On the way back, they grabbed dinner from a Chinese take-out and ate chicken chow mein and shrimp fried rice while watching a Sunday evening sitcom on TV. Both of them refrained from discussing the case, but it wasn't far from either one of their minds.

Emotionally exhausted from the day's events, Paige didn't bother to smother a huge yawn. "I think it's time for bed," she said to Josh, who sat on the couch a few feet away from her.

"I agree." He sounded just as tired, though he appeared wide-awake and alert. Standing, he picked up the remote, clicked off the TV, and started toward the foyer. "You go on and change, and I'll make sure everything is locked up."

Grateful for the security of Josh's presence, Paige went to her bedroom and hesitated just inside the doorway. The room that had become a haven for her since Anthony's death, a place to unwind and pamper herself, had changed since that morning—not in appearance, but in *feel*. The very air around her seemed tainted by a man's ruthless quest for wealth. As she stood there and considered that the house and its rich, luxurious contents most likely had been purchased with stolen money, an ominous cast settled over the entire dwelling.

A shiver chased down her spine, cold and unwelcome. Forcing those unpleasant thoughts from her head and replacing them with firm resolve, she headed into the bathroom, pinned up her hair, and took a long, hot shower. Tomorrow, she'd begin the proceedings that would rid her of the disturbing memories this house evoked. Tomorrow, she'd make the first step toward her future, and a new life away from Miami.

Twenty minutes later she exited the bathroom wearing her favorite lavender chemise, ready to crawl in between soft, cool sheets and forget the past twenty-four hours in lieu of a good, solid eight hours of much-needed sleep.

She came to a jarring stop in the middle of the room.

Josh stood at the opposite side of her four-poster bed, in the process of stripping off his clothes. His shirt was gone, and her insidious pulse raced at the sight of his well-defined chest, his lean belly and narrow hips—hot, naked skin she'd stroked with her hands and tasted with her lips the night before. Long fingers worked at the belt buckle at his waist, his movements slow and unhurried, as if he belonged in her room, in her bed, under her skin....

And for a timeless moment the intimate scene seemed so normal, so perfectly right...until her gaze touched on the weapon resting on the nightstand next to him, bringing everything back into perspective...for all of five seconds.

He glanced up, his warm, golden-brown gaze leisurely sliding down the length of her, a sensual visual caress that stole the breath from her lungs. There was nothing suggestive, revealing, or provocative about the nightgown she wore, nothing to inspire the primitive hunger and raw desire reflected in his expression, yet she felt undeniably sexy, incredibly voluptuous, and very aware of herself as a woman. The gauzy material should have been cool against her skin, yet the fabric seemed to singe the tips of her breasts as it brushed across her nipples. The crests peaked, tightened, and ached for the slow, wet attention he'd given them last night with his mouth. Her heart hammered, her stomach tumbled, and the insides of her thighs tingled in an arousing way.

She'd never considered herself an overtly sexual creature. She'd only been with two men before Anthony, and none of them, not even her own husband, had ever come close to making her unravel and melt with a mere look. None had ever made her want to do the shameless, erotic things she wanted to do with the man in front of her.

With Josh, the awareness was all the more tempting and seductive because she'd experienced just how thrilling making love with him could be—how *satisfying*, emotionally and physically. That intrinsic connection was like touching a live wire, and just as dangerous to her heart.

He lifted his gaze, meeting hers, a wicked, unapologetic gleam in his eyes. He'd purposely made her burn, she realized. Deliberately seduced her without touching her at all. That effortless, intimate influence he held over her was unnerving; his presumptuousness in being in her bedroom annoyed her.

Finally, she found her voice. "What are you doing in here?"

"I thought that was fairly obvious." His fingers unsnapped his jeans, and his mouth quirked in a half smile that was both mischievous and challenging. "I'm getting ready for bed."

The rasp of his jeans' zipper filled the room, and her faithless body swelled in anticipation. "In here? With me?" She sounded prim and haughty, but didn't care.

Neither did he. The humor glimmering to life in his eyes expressed his disregard. "Yes, in here. With you."

She moved toward the bed, trying to maintain a semblance of calm when she was feeling entirely too reckless. She clearly remembered what had happened in this bed with him in the darkest hours of the night, how she'd woken to feel the heat of his body along the back of hers as he claimed her in such a primitive way.

She couldn't risk letting that happen again, and refused to make their situation any more complicated than it already was. "What's wrong with the couch in the living room?"

"Too far away if something should happen during the night." As if his statement ended the discussion, he hooked his fingers into the waistband of his jeans and pushed the denim over his hips and down his long, muscular legs. Just like that, he shucked his pants. Just like that, he stood before her in nothing more than a pair of sexy, white briefs that hugged impressive male anatomy in a state of semiarousal.

She jerked her gaze up, preferring the relatively safe territory of his bare chest. "Letting you stay here and pretend to be my lover to protect me is one thing, but sleeping in the same bed wasn't part of the plan."

"Tonight, it's strictly business." He tossed the frilly pillows aside and pulled down the covers. "And it's not as though we haven't slept in the same bed before."

A flood of warmth suffused her cheeks at his blatant reference to last night, but she refused to give in. She jutted her chin stubbornly. "Last night was... different."

Irritation touched his features, and for a moment she thought he was going to argue and tell her that last night wasn't any different than tonight, that the desire and need was still shimmering between them.

But he didn't say any of what they both already knew. Giving his head a shake, he ignored her feeble

protests and slid in between the sheets and covers.
"C'mon to bed, Paige," he said, giving the pillow beside him a light pat. "I'm dead tired after today, and I
swear I don't have a lascivious thought in my head."

His mouth recited the lie easily, but his gaze was far
more honest. Those rich brown eyes said he wanted
her, but they also reassured her that he'd respect her
wishes and wouldn't touch her except to protect her.
Believing him, and trusting him, she didn't issue any
further objection.

She set her alarm for 6:00 a.m., turned off the lights
and crawled into bed. As she lay there in the darkness
listening to the odd night sounds from outside, she admitted to herself that she was glad he'd insisted on staying in the bedroom with her. Not only did she not want
to be alone, but he made her feel safe and secure.

Within ten minutes Josh was asleep, his breathing
deep and even. She spent what seemed like hours tossing and turning. Every time she closed her eyes or
started to drift off, images of last night stole into her
mind, making her ache, making her restless and
aroused. And despite every valid reason not to, she
wanted to feel Josh inside her again, filling her, giving
her everything her body and soul hungered for.

He kept his promise and stayed on his side of the
bed. Didn't so much as allow an arm or leg to cross the
halfway mark. She should have been glad, but resented
his willpower when it appeared she had none.

Gritting her teeth, she rolled to her side, facing the
gorgeous man sleeping so peacefully beside her. A man
who'd given her so much and had asked for so little in
return. A man she'd fallen in love with, but who was all
wrong for her for so many different reasons.

She reached out to touch his chest. Halfway there she

curled her hand into a fist and pulled it back, knowing she'd only be inviting trouble and complications she didn't need if she allowed her emotions to interfere with the important decisions she'd made.

A lump formed in her throat, followed by stinging tears, which she valiantly tried to blink back. God, she was so confused and torn about her feelings for Josh— this almost desperate need she had for him—and about her decision to leave him as soon as circumstances allowed.

It couldn't be any other way. She refused to let her heart overrule her head this time, refused to give herself to another man who lived on the edge of danger and risked his life on a daily basis. She swallowed thickly and valiantly tried not to think of the possibility of being pregnant with Josh's child, or how that would irrevocably change the plans she'd set for her future.

Somewhere between midnight and the edge of dawn she finally slipped into a deep, exhausted sleep—but her dreams were of Josh, and the emptiness of living without him.

PAIGE GLANCED out the passenger window of her Volvo as Josh drove her to the Wild Rose the next morning. When she'd asked if she could drive herself while he followed in his Thunderbird, he'd told her that they'd be using her car until the case was over, since he didn't want to chance someone tracing his license plate. She'd been unable to argue with his logic, and his vehicle was now parked safely in his garage. He'd be escorting her to and from work, or anywhere else she requested. End of discussion.

As much as she appreciated Josh keeping her safe and protected, she hated depending on him, and disliked the complete control he seemed to have over her life. It reminded her too much of Anthony's dominating, manipulative ways.

She knew this predicament was different from her marriage, and temporary, but that didn't make her despise the situation, or her dependence on Josh, any less. Her privacy was a thing of the past, and being under twenty-four-hour surveillance made it difficult to sort out thoughts, feelings and decisions that were becoming increasingly more tangled and complex.

Paige nearly jumped out of her skin when Josh reached across the center console and rested a hand on her knee, just below the hem of her navy skirt. Damn. If his purpose was to get her attention, he certainly had it.

"You're awfully quiet this morning," he commented, his deep voice filling the interior of the vehicle with rich male tones, made more intimate by the close confines of the car. "Did you sleep okay?"

His thumb absently stroked the outside of her thigh, and Paige's nerves screamed in awareness. What once would have been construed as an innocent, comforting gesture now caused excitement to ripple through her. And the most disconcerting thing was, she liked the sensation and enjoyed his caresses. Now that she knew the kind of intense pleasure Josh was capable of giving her, her body seemed to crave his touch, and responded to it eagerly.

She dragged in a deep, steadying breath in an effort to rein in her provocative thoughts. "I slept wonderfully," she lied, unwilling to share just how restless her night had been, or how flustered and aroused she was currently feeling, all from his touch. "I just have a lot of things on my mind."

A lazy smile curved his mouth, but his expression reflected the warmth and care she'd always cherished with their friendship. "Such as?"

What I'm going to do about our relationship now that we've crossed that line and become lovers, and how incredibly difficult it's going to be to keep from making love to you again. "Things I need to get done at the boutique today."

He nodded, and finally lifted his hand from her leg as he drove through an intersection, allowing her to breathe easier. "I spoke with Reynolds early this morning, and he's set up a female undercover officer to meet us at the Wild Rose. Her name is Liz Forster, and not only is she a dedicated cop, she comes at the expense of the department. Feel free to put her to work."

She crossed a leg over the burning imprint left by his hand. The swish of silk on silk echoed in the vehicle, sounding incredibly sensual to her own ears. "I couldn't possibly do that."

"You need to treat her like a civilian, Paige." He made a turn onto Harding Avenue, where her shop was located along Surfside's main commercial drag. "She's a decoy, there to protect you when I'm not around, but she needs to look like just another employee. That means you or your assistant should train her accordingly, so she blends in." His firm tone brooked no argument.

"All right," she agreed as he pulled her car into a vacant parking slot in front of the Wild Rose and cut the engine. The dress shop was located between a chic hair salon and a quaint coffeehouse, which gave her a nice overflow of tourists to supplement the local patrons who frequented her boutique. "I suppose I can keep her busy helping Pam rearrange the front window display."

"Whatever you need, she'll do, as long as you stick nearby." He turned toward her, his expression granite hard. "If you leave the shop, for *anything*, she goes with you. Is that clear?"

Remembering his stern lecture yesterday on the beach, and the possible repercussions of venturing out alone, she tried not to let her resentment of the situation overrule common sense. "Crystal clear."

"Good," he said, satisfied with her acquiescence.

Grabbing her briefcase and slinging the long strap of her purse over her shoulder, she exited the car. Josh met her on the sidewalk, looking casually handsome in a pair of black jeans and a beige and black patterned knit shirt overlaid with a black leather bomber jacket— which concealed the gun secured in his shoulder holster. He didn't look like a detective, but the gorgeous rebel who supposedly was her lover.

He eased into the role effortlessly. Sliding his hand into her free one, he wove their fingers intimately together. Paige's pulse tripped all over itself at his brazen, possessive display, and she tugged her hand back, but to no avail.

"Relax, Paige," he murmured, bestowing a dazzling, loverlike smile on her. "And act natural."

"Taking on a lover is hardly an everyday occurrence for me," she said in a low, heated voice while smiling to Janice, the woman who owned the hair salon next to her shop and was currently eyeballing the two of them with interest.

"If anybody questions the employees in the shops around yours I'd like them to be able to verify that you're seeing someone."

She understood his purpose, she truly did, but she hated broadcasting that she and Josh had actually become lovers. Especially when she was desperately trying to put their relationship back into proper perspective, which didn't include the illusion of having an affair.

Since they were early, Josh hung out for half an hour, passing the time by strolling around the boutique filled with women's clothing, lingerie and accessories while Paige counted out the cash drawer and readied the shop for the day.

Liz arrived first, surprising Paige by looking exactly like the kind of sophisticated salesperson she herself would have hired for the Wild Rose. The young woman was tall and slender—not at all the muscular type Paige had anticipated—and was dressed immaculately in an outfit that could have been selected from Paige's own inventory: cream slacks, a rose-hued silk blouse with a light, linen jacket, and fashionable leather pumps. Liz's rich, sable hair was cut into a short, chic style that emphasized her pretty features and striking blue eyes.

Paige immediately felt comfortable with the other woman, who was friendly and outgoing, despite the grimness of her occupation and the seriousness surrounding her current assignment. When Paige jokingly commented that Liz looked about as intimidating as a butterfly, Josh assured her that Liz was well trained, and one of the best female undercover officers they had in the department.

Pam entered the Wild Rose shortly after Liz, and because she'd been with Paige from the day she'd opened the boutique, and Paige trusted her implicitly, Josh briefed the younger woman on the situation. He skimmed the more dangerous, relevant details he'd shared with Paige, explaining just enough for Pam to understand the need for Paige to be guarded, yet not enough to put her own life at risk for knowing too much.

By the time Josh was ready to leave, Paige was ready to see him go. Her stomach was in knots, and the beginnings of a headache throbbed at her temples. This entire scenario had her feeling cornered, edgy and irritable. She walked with him just outside the boutique, and they stood beneath the awning above the shop.

"I've got a lot to take care of today on the case," Josh said, retrieving her car keys from the front pocket of his black jeans. "I'll be back at closing time to pick you up."

She crossed her arms over her chest. "So, you're leaving me here without a vehicle?"

"If you need to go anywhere, Liz will take you. That's what she's here for."

She opened her mouth to issue a mild objection out of pure defiance. At the same moment, he curled a hand around the back of her neck and brought her lips to his. He kissed her, taking advantage of her parted lips to boldly slide his tongue inside her mouth. The kiss was quick, but hot, shockingly erotic, and extremely possessive. The emotional impact shook Paige to the core, made her melt against him when she knew she should make some attempt to push him away.

He ended the kiss, and she was horrified to hear a whimper of protest purr from her throat. He looked extremely pleased with himself, cocky and arrogant and triumphant.

She straightened away, grasping for her composure. "Was that necessary?" she asked primly.

His grin was unapologetic. "Oh, yeah, it was," he said huskily, unmistakable desire brightening his eyes. "Not only have I had the urge to kiss you the past two days, but to anyone who might be watching, like that nosy lady in the hair shop next door, we look like legitimate lovers."

She was in trouble, she realized, instinctively knowing that kiss had been more than a charade. It was meant as a reminder of the intimacy they'd shared—one he wasn't about to let her forget.

He brushed his knuckles down her cheek in a loving caress at odds with the sudden seriousness of his gaze. "Now go back inside and be good for Liz."

The order made her bristle, but she obeyed. There was no point starting an argument with Josh while they had an audience. Without so much as a goodbye, she went back into the boutique and headed to her office to take care of the most important business she had on her agenda. Setting her briefcase on her rolltop oak desk, she opened it and searched for the file she needed.

"So, you finally hooked up with Josh, huh?"

Paige glanced up sharply from her task, watching as Pam entered her office. Other than Josh, Pam was one of the closest friends she had in Miami, though she'd shared very few of her marital problems with the other woman. However, considering that the rare times Pam had met Anthony he'd been hostile, rude and hardly a loving husband, it wouldn't have been difficult for anyone to deduce that her relationship with Anthony had been strained. But for Pam to make a comment about her and Josh was a little unsettling.

"It's not what it seems." Finding the folder she needed, she set her briefcase back on the mauve carpeting beside her desk. "That kiss you witnessed is just a pretense," she said, striving for a vagueness she didn't quite feel, not when that breath-stealing embrace still had her heart pumping faster than normal. "Nothing more."

"Uh-huh," Pam said, her expression doubtful. "But it didn't seem like either one of you had to pretend *too* much."

"Excuse me?" she croaked, praying that her feelings for Josh hadn't been so obvious from just a kiss.

Her prayers went unanswered. "There's always been something between you and Josh, a rare kind of chemistry you don't see between two people very often."

Oh, God. "You know, this is something I'd rather not discuss." It was bad enough that she was feeling a subtle pressure from Josh; she didn't need it from Pam, too.

"I understand." Pam smiled and shrugged. "I just thought you'd finally realized that the guy is absolutely crazy about you."

Paige knew. Her chest burned with the knowledge. Oh, Lord, Josh had made his feelings and intentions plain with every touch, every word, every action since the night they'd made love.

He is completely and totally wrong for me, she wanted to explain. *He's a cop, a man more dedicated to his job than he ever could be to me or a family.*

But her biggest fears remained lodged in her throat, and Pam finally left her office, closing the door behind her. And because she knew that she had no future with Josh, that to remain in Miami would only cause her more heartache, she flipped open the file folder and searched for the business card she'd tucked in there a few weeks ago.

Then she reached for the phone and forced herself to dial the Realtor's phone number.

5

JOSH BROUGHT Paige's Volvo to an abrupt stop in the driveway of her beach house. On some level, he acknowledged that the For Sale sign posted on the front lawn shouldn't have come as a surprise considering the revelations of the past week, but he was more than a little irritated that she hadn't thought to share this momentous decision with him.

The woman sitting in the passenger seat next to him stared straight ahead, waiting for him to park the car in the garage, as was their nightly routine. She looked poised and distant, as if putting her house up for sale was nothing out of the ordinary.

His world had ceased being ordinary the night she'd asked him to make love to her. Everything she did, every decision she made, now affected the way his life, his future, would evolve. Apparently, she didn't feel the same, and that provoked his temper. Her indifference *had* to be a farce. A woman didn't give herself to a man the way Paige had so passionately offered herself to him without establishing some kind of emotional bond.

Keeping a tight rein on his darkening mood so he didn't say or do something he'd regret later, he let the car roll forward into the garage. Before he could shut down the engine, Paige slipped out of the vehicle without a word, her purse and briefcase in hand. She

pressed a code on the keypad on the wall that unlocked
the door leading into the house and disabled the alarm.
With a gentle sway of her hips beneath that coral-hued,
straight-line knit dress she wore, she stepped inside,
leaving the door open for him to follow.

Blowing out a harsh breath, he exited the car, shut the
rolling garage door, and strode into the house in search
of Paige. Judging by her hasty retreat, he knew she
planned on avoiding him and the inevitable discussion
ahead. He'd allowed her to maintain her distance since
Monday, hadn't pressured her the past three days for
more than she was willing to give. He'd acted as professional and courteous as his job required, catering to her
remote behavior and putting his own needs aside.

Not this time. As he followed the sounds drifting
from the kitchen, he discovered he was itching for a
confrontation. He wanted answers, and he intended to
get them. He wanted to know where he stood with her.
The evening wouldn't end until he found out.

In the kitchen, Paige was pouring herself a glass of
wine. It was an evening ritual—one glass of chardon-
nay, retreating to her bedroom for a long bath and to
change, a quiet dinner, about an hour of TV, then bed.

He was tired of the monotony. Tired of avoiding important issues that affected both of their lives. Tired of
lying in bed at night beside her—so close, so tempting—yet unable to pull her soft, responsive body beneath his as he longed to.

Tossing the keys onto the counter, he let his frustration get the best of him. "Why didn't you tell me you
listed the house?"

She stiffened at his demanding question, though she
didn't turn around and look at him. With incredibly
steady hands, she recorked the bottle of wine, slipped it

back into the refrigerator, and returned to the glass she'd left on the counter. "I wasn't aware that I needed your permission to put the house up for sale."

He jammed his hands on his hips, not that his fierce stance had much chance of intimidating the woman who stood with her back to him, looking out the kitchen window as she took a sip of wine. "That isn't what I meant, and you know it," he said in a low voice.

Her shoulders lifted in a nonchalant shrug. "I didn't think selling *my* house was any of your concern."

Not any of his concern? Her sharp-edged comment hit below the belt, prompting a fury that boiled just beneath the surface of his skin—until he recognized her defense tactic. Enough words, he wanted to see her eyes. They'd never lied to him before. "Dammit, Paige, *look at me.*"

She turned around, chin up, her auburn hair swinging sassily along her shoulders with the defiant movement. Vibrant green eyes glared in reply to his gruff command, but there was something else beyond the anger, a heart-deep misery he'd seen too many times in the past to dismiss. An emotion that never failed to make his protective instincts come alive.

This tense moment was no different, but as much as he wanted to reach out and touch her, he knew she wouldn't welcome the connection. He wanted answers, needed to know her reasons for making such a crucial decision that affected both of their lives, possibly even their future together. He *had* to know what her intentions were.

Treading cautiously, he said quietly, "Why are you selling the house?"

"You have to ask, after everything that's happened the past week?" Her tone was high-pitched and incredulous. Before he could respond, she continued, "Not only does this place now make me feel uncomfortable, but it was always Anthony's house, never mine. He designed and furnished it before I became part of his life." She dragged her hand through her hair, pushing it away from her face. Her eyes looked huge, her features weary. "And it's too big for one person. The upkeep is more than I need right now."

Relief coursed through him. Her rationalization made perfect sense, of course. He'd read too much into the sign out front, had reacted without knowing the facts, which wasn't like him at all. "I'd be more than happy to help you find something else. Maybe a nice condo that's closer to the Wild Rose."

"Josh..." Looking away again, she dampened her bottom lip with her tongue, and continued on a rush of breath, "I put the Wild Rose up for sale, too."

Josh's entire universe shifted, and his heart slammed painfully against his ribs. He didn't like where this conversation was heading, or what her decisions implied. He kept a casual attitude, though he was feeling anything but. "Why would you want to sell the Wild Rose? Your shop is one of the most successful boutiques on Harding Avenue."

"Yeah, it's done quite well in the two years I've had it," she agreed, a small, satisfied smile playing around the corners of her mouth. "And it helped me keep my sanity. Without it, I would have gone crazy with boredom. But like my marriage to Anthony, the Wild Rose is a piece of my life I'd rather put behind me. I've lived, I've learned, and as soon as this case of yours is over, I'm moving on, a wiser person," she said, reciting her father's quote. Lifting her glass of wine from the counter, she headed out of the kitchen and through the living room, putting an end to their conversation.

Standing there in the silence, he thought about all she'd said, and what she *hadn't* said. Deciding he wasn't going to let the subject drop so easily, not when he didn't have a firm grasp on her intentions, he stalked after her. Ignoring the closed bedroom door, he barged into her room unannounced.

She stood by the dresser. She'd just kicked off her heels and was in the process of unbuttoning the front of her dress. Visibly startled by his bold intrusion, she gasped, then scowled at him. "Do you mind, Josh? I'd like a little privacy."

"Oh, I mind all right," he murmured as he moved toward her, his gaze riveted to the five buttons she'd opened, low enough to reveal the scalloped edges of a lacy bra, and the firm upper slopes of her breasts. He forced himself to drag his eyes from that enticement before he forgot his purpose for seeking her out. "You walked away before we were done talking."

She watched him invade her room, wariness glimmering in the depths of her eyes. "There's not a whole lot left to say."

He stopped an arm's length away and saw the pulse at the base of her throat flutter nervously. "You left out a little detail."

"Oh?" A delicate brow arched. "And what was that?" She took a subtle step to the side, as if he stood too close, crowding her personal space. As if she wanted clearance to bolt...

He wasn't about to give her the chance. Calculating her next move, he shifted the weight of his body accordingly, letting her know without words that there would be no escaping him, or their conversation.

"Moving on to *where*, Paige?" His voice was soft, deceptively so.

Since she couldn't dart around him, she turned away, hiding her expression and those luminous eyes that radiated her deepest emotions. Slipping off the bracelet made of incandescent beads that complemented the color of her dress, she set it on the dresser, then removed the matching earrings. Very quietly, she said, "I've decided to move back home to Connecticut, so I can be near my family."

Outwardly, Josh accepted her bombshell with admirable calm. Inwardly, however, panic spread through him, sending his pulse racing.

He didn't want to lose Paige!

But you never really had her, the rational part of his mind argued. Even though his feelings for her had developed into something stronger and deeper than friendship, they'd made no personal commitment to each other, nothing to indicate they had any kind of future together. All they had was one incredible night of passion....

He grasped for leverage, focusing on the one thing that would drastically change both of their lives. "And what if you're pregnant with my baby?"

She whirled around, startled, eyes wide. Her hand fluttered to her flat belly, and when she realized what she'd done, she quickly jerked it away. "I'm not pregnant," she said firmly.

"Oh?" His tone challenged. "Have you started your period?"

She hesitated, but in the end couldn't lie. "Not yet."

"The day after we made love you said you were due to start soon." He studied her intently. "Are you regular?"

Her face flushed, whether in embarrassment or annoyance at his persistence, he wasn't sure. "I haven't been regular since I went off the Pill when Anthony died," she admitted. "But I know my body, and I'm not pregnant."

He wondered who she was trying to convince—him or herself.

She moved past him, while he digested what she'd just told him. She opened the glass slider leading to the deck that wrapped around the house, leaving the screen door locked and secured. A cool evening breeze blew in, circulating fresh air through the room. The low rumbling of waves breaking along the shore echoed in the distance, the sound tranquil and soothing.

He came up beside her, his mood calmer than before. He'd gotten most of the answers he'd wanted, but another still niggled, and he voiced it. "You were on the Pill while you were married?"

She glanced at him, a droll smile lifting one corner of her mouth. "That's not something a woman broadcasts, Marchiano, even to a good friend."

He shook his head, realizing she'd misconstrued his meaning. "You talked about having kids and a family, and I just assumed you would have welcomed a pregnancy."

"I'm afraid that was wishful thinking on my part. During our first year of marriage a huge part of me thought a baby would make Anthony settle down, make him less reckless...." Her voice trailed off. After a moment, her gaze flickered to his, her expression etched with the same unhappiness that had shadowed the last two years of her marriage. "About nine months after we married, Anthony insisted I go on the Pill. He claimed he wasn't ready for kids and he didn't want to risk an 'accident.' Looking back, going on the Pill was a blessing in disguise, considering the life-style Anthony led outside of our marriage. I'm grateful I don't have children to worry about right now, and I sure as heck wouldn't want to have to explain that their father was a criminal."

A light gust filtered through the screen, sifting through her hair and tugging gently at the light material of her dress, molding the fabric to her curves. Josh envied that clinging dress, wished it were his hands shaping her firm, generous breasts, skimming over the swell of her hips, grazing the length of her slender thighs....

"What about the possibility of having *my* baby?" he asked, his voice low and husky.

"That would only complicate matters, Josh." She released an agitated sigh and paced back into the bedroom. "I'm leaving as soon as things are wrapped up here in Miami. I miss my family, and I miss the simplicity of a small town. It's where I belong. It's where I've *always* belonged." She abruptly stopped beside her four-poster bed, imploring him to understand. "I'm not cut out for the city, the crime, or being a cop's wife. If I was too naive to know that when I married Anthony, I certainly realize it now."

Josh felt that an integral part of his life was crumbling right before his eyes. "Maybe you just need more time before you make a big decision like this," he suggested, anything to buy time for her to reconsider her options. Options that included him being a part of her life. Options that didn't include her moving to another state. "It's only been three months since Anthony died. I know how difficult things have been lately, especially this past week—"

"My mind is made up, Josh," she said adamantly, exercising that stubborn streak he both admired and disliked at the moment. "There's nothing left for me here but bad memories."

Fast as lightning, he shot back, "Am *I* nothing but a bad memory?"

His blunt question startled her. Then her gaze softened and she reached out and pressed her hand to his cheek, her touch warm and infinitely gentle. "You, Josh, have become one of my best friends, and I care for you more than you'll ever know," she whispered in a tight, aching voice. "I honestly don't know what I would have done without you these past three years."

Incensed beyond reason, he grasped her wrist and pulled her hand away, ignoring her startled catch of breath. Goddammit, he wanted more than cordiality and appreciation. More than her gratitude for being around when Anthony hadn't been, for giving her the affection her own husband had been too self-centered to offer. He wanted her to acknowledge that they meant more to each other than just *friends*.

"Josh?"

Her voice trembled with uncertainty. He knew he should let her go and end this craziness, but he had a desperate, overwhelming need to prove that what they'd spent three years nurturing deserved a fair chance to develop into something deeper and more intimate than what they already shared.

With a vicious curse, he plowed his free hand into her hair, cradled the back of her head in his palm, and lifted her mouth to his. She tensed and tried to turn away at the last second, but she was no match for his strength, or the need that coursed through his blood. Their lips touched, melded, fused. He wouldn't accept anything less. His tongue was just as relentless, gliding deep within her mouth to claim, conquer and cajole her compliance.

Then, even that wasn't enough. He wanted her total surrender. Wanted to brand her, remind her how sweetly she responded to him, how hot and needy she became beneath his touch.

Still holding her, still kissing her, he guided her backwards, until the edge of the mattress clipped the back of her legs and she had no choice but to tumble onto the bed. He swallowed her gasp as he followed her down, ignored her feeble struggles as he pushed her higher onto the mattress and wedged a hard, muscular thigh between her knees.

Her one free hand gripped his shirt—to pull him close or push him away, he wasn't sure. In an attempt to eliminate the latter possibility, he untangled his fingers from her silky hair, disengaged her hand from his shirt, and single-handedly pinned it with the other above her head.

Only then did he end that endlessly long, thorough kiss. They were both breathing hard, trying to recover from that wild, dizzying ride. She tugged weakly on her manacled wrists, but he wasn't done seducing her. No, not even close.

His fingers skillfully, effortlessly, flicked open three more buttons on her dress while his open mouth discovered a soft, ultrasensitive spot along her throat that made her shiver. His tongue skimmed a path to her ear where he murmured his intentions in explicitly shocking detail.

"No," she moaned, a paltry protest her mouth, her body, didn't agree with. Her lips were wet, parted, and lush, receiving his rapacious kisses and returning them with equal fervor. Her body twisted sensually toward his for something more.

"Oh, yes," he breathed hotly, burying his face in the warm, fragrant curve of her neck. His fingers unsnapped the front closure of her satin-and-lace bra and pushed the cups aside, baring her to him. He filled his large palm with her plump flesh, grazed his thumb across a nipple until it grew pebble-hard.

The moment he touched her, she yielded to his caress, grew pliant and just as needy as he. In the depths of her heavy-lidded eyes he saw her succumb, felt her body release all tension and soften with feminine allure.

That was all the urging it took for him to proceed in making good on the promises he'd whispered in her ear. He dragged his mouth along her collarbone, laved warm, damp kisses on her chest, nipped gently at the slope of her breasts until they swelled and tightened. His tongue lavished the crests with attention, flicking teasingly, lapping temptingly, until finally he drew her nipple deep within his mouth and suckled hungrily.

A helpless sob caught in her throat, and the hands he'd restrained above her head curled into tight fists, though she didn't struggle. Her breathing deepened, grew ragged and labored with an unspoken need he understood. His own body hardened, his erection pressing insistently against her thigh. For as much as he wanted to be inside her sleek, giving warmth, tonight, the pleasure was all hers.

His free hand explored, trailing a burning path over her hip, down her thigh, then swept beneath the hem of her dress. His questing fingertips rasped along silky stockings, sending his blood soaring. As he skimmed higher, stroking the inside of her thighs, her legs gradually, instinctively relaxed and eased apart for him. He had no idea what he'd expected to find, but the delicate lace band holding up her stockings was a delightful and arousing surprise. The three inches of bare skin he caressed next was baby-soft and quivering. And then he reached her panties, a satiny scrap of fabric covering her most feminine secrets. He stroked his fingers along the exquisitely sensitive flesh hidden beneath the flimsy barrier, and experienced supreme satisfaction when heat and dampness greeted his touch.

Her entire body shuddered at the intimate caress, and her hips rolled upward, seeking a deeper contact. "Josh, please…" she whispered raggedly.

Lifting his mouth from her breasts, he looked up at her face, flushed with sensual longing. Her eyes were bright and fevered and unfocused. She looked beautiful, and damn exciting, spread so wantonly beneath him.

"Please what?" he murmured, refusing to give her what her body craved unless she admitted her desire and need for him. "Tell me what you want, and I'll give it to you."

She bit her bottom lip and moaned in frustration. Then, seemingly unable to deny her need for him, she told him exactly what she wanted. "Touch me…kiss me…" *Love me*, her eyes begged.

He touched her, watching her slowly unravel as he pushed aside the elastic band of her panties, eased a finger inside her, and slicked his thumb along petal-soft folds of flesh.

He lowered his head and kissed her, a slow, languid melding of lips and tongue that matched the sensual rhythm of his fingers.

Loving her was the easiest part of all; his feelings came naturally, from the depths of his heart and soul.

In the next instant she gave him what he ultimately wanted. Her climax was powerful and emotional, making her shudder and cry out for him as the waves of pure, blissful fulfillment engulfed her. When it was over and Paige's body ceased quivering, Josh released her hands and rested his head just above her breasts, absorbing the wild beating of her heart that echoed the racing of his pulse. His own body throbbed, but this moment wasn't about his pleasure and surrender, but hers.

She knew it, too. "Damn you, Josh," she said in a low, fierce tone that expressed her anger at the situation, and herself.

He chuckled lightly, and her nipple tightened as his breath caressed the tip. "Those weren't quite the words of gratitude I was hoping for."

She twined her fingers in his hair, forcing him to lift his head and look at her. "You're an arrogant bastard."

He grew serious, opting for honesty instead of humor. "When it comes to you, yeah, I probably am. I want you to think about everything you'll be leaving behind if you move back to Connecticut."

"Great sex?" she asked flippantly.

His mouth thinned in annoyance. "What's between us is more than sex, as hot and fantastic as it is. You know that, even if you won't admit it." He smoothed her hair away from her face, the gesture more an excuse to touch her than anything else. "I can't make the bad memories go away, but I can replace them with good memories if you'll just give me the chance."

"It's not that simple." Untangling her fingers from his hair, she moved from beside him and sat on the edge of the mattress. She tugged at the sides of her dress, covering her breasts. "It's not only about us, or Anthony, but who and what you are, too."

"A cop," he said flatly, finally understanding.

She nodded, her expression regretful. "Unfortunately, yes."

He stood and dragged a hand through his tousled hair. His body was tense from the arousal still thrumming through his veins, and from Paige's stubborn ideas. "I'm a homicide detective, Paige," he said, trying to reason with her. "Not a vice cop like Anthony was."

"The danger is still there, so is the risk. The gun you wear proves that. This *case* we're both involved in proves it." Her argument was fierce and heated, spurred by her own personal experience. "I can't go through that again. I want a husband I can count on coming home at night. I want a stable, wholesome environment for my children. And if that's selfish of me, then so be it."

He chose his rebuttal carefully. "I don't think it's at all selfish to want those things. But I also know it's possible to be married to a cop and have a good, stable home life. My parents are proof of that. You've met them and can see for yourself how happy they are together. And I don't think any one of their five kids suffered because my father was a cop."

Her chin shot up. "And how many times do you think your mother stayed up all night long while your father was out on patrol or working on a case, wondering if he was going to come home in the morning? Or if she'd find his partner at the door to inform her that her husband had been killed in the line of duty?"

Her bitter memories were difficult to compete with. "I'm sure, in a lot of ways, my mother felt exactly the way you did." He'd heard enough complaints from colleagues about the strain their job put on their marriages, many of which didn't survive the pressure, to know the problem was prevalent in law enforcement. But buckling under the stress didn't happen to everyone. "My father is a good man, Paige, loyal and scrupulous to a fault. Those traits are what matters when it comes to his devotion to his wife and family. It's the difference between me and Anthony."

She shook her head and whispered, "I can't do it again, Josh." Standing, she headed for the adjoining bathroom.

Desperation gripped him, and he cut straight into her path, halting her. "Paige—"

She pressed her fingers to his lips, cutting off any further debate. Tears welled in her eyes, and her bottom lip quivered. "Don't make this any harder than it already is, okay, Josh?"

She didn't wait for an answer. Stepping around him, she sequestered herself in the bathroom. After a moment, the sound of running water filling the sunken tub broke the silence.

Sighing heavily, Josh dropped back onto the bed and scrubbed a hand over his face, mentally berating himself for being such an idiot. Christ, what a mess he'd made of things. He'd pushed Paige before she was ready, and although she'd yielded to his physical seduction, he now realized the emotional scars her husband had inflicted were a long way from healing.

After the hell Anthony put Paige through, Josh was seriously beginning to wonder if he had the right to make his own selfish demands.

WORK WAS her only refuge. Paige welcomed the afternoon diversion of helping Liz unpack a new shipment

of spring outfits, accessories and lingerie and putting
them on display. Too soon, Josh would arrive to whisk
her back to the beach house where she'd have to endure
another long, tense evening of polite talk with a man
she'd never before had any trouble conversing with—
until her life had been turned upside down.

Between Liz's surveillance at the boutique, and Josh
shadowing her the rest of the time, she was feeling
cooped up and boxed in. If she wanted solitude, she escaped to the bathroom, and even then she'd learned if
she exceeded the paranoid cops' time limit, they rapped
on the door for a response, shattering the private moment.

Liz accompanied her to lunch every day, and to run
errands and do the banking. The woman was never
more than a scream away, and though she had a lively
personality and appeared slender and unsubstantial,
beneath the facade, Liz was one tough officer. Per Josh's
instructions, during lulls in business Liz had taken
Paige into the office and taught her basic self-defense
maneuvers. Paige had been awed by Liz's strength and
agility, and the variety of ways a woman could disable
a man if the need arose.

Ultimately, Paige couldn't wait to get this entire mess
over with. Couldn't wait to resume a normal life. And
in that vein, she'd called her sister, Valerie, earlier that
morning to touch bases and chat, needing that familial
connection she'd missed so much the past three years.
While she couldn't give her sibling an exact day for her
homecoming, she'd promised Valerie she'd be returning to Connecticut soon. Not wanting to worry her sister, or her parents, she refrained from mentioning her
current predicament, or the danger her life was in.

"Wow, would you take a look at this stuff?" Liz exclaimed excitedly as she pulled a froth of silk and lace from a box she'd just opened. Satiny jeweled tones in amethyst, emerald, sapphire and ruby shimmered beneath the overhead lights and slid through her fingers like quicksilver. "These nightgowns are gorgeous, and so sexy! How am I going to choose just one color?"

Paige laughed, enjoying Liz's enthusiasm, and the diversion from her thoughts. It hadn't taken long for Paige to realize that Liz was a clotheshorse at heart, and her current assignment allowed her to indulge the habit on a daily basis. "Well, you could always buy one of each."

"You're absolutely no help to my addiction," she complained good-naturedly. Holding up a sapphire gown to her slim figure, she gazed thoughtfully at her reflection in the mirror, located in the back storeroom, where they tagged merchandise before putting it out on the floor. "Before this case is over, I'm going to have to sign my month's salary over to you."

Paige smiled as she attached price tags to the lingerie. "But you're going to look absolutely fabulous." And at an excellent price, too, since Paige had offered Liz the employee thirty-percent discount as compensation for actually working at the boutique while she was on assignment. Paige wanted to do something for the other woman, who'd proved her worth as an employee, as well as a guardian, and the savings seemed to thrill Liz.

"Oh, and I just have to have one of these," she said, putting aside a teddy designed in cream satin and french lace. Her blue eyes twinkled merrily. "There's nothing that feels sexier than silk and lace against your skin or beneath your clothes. And my boyfriend enjoys the surprise, too," she added with a wink.

"Looks like he's got quite a few surprises coming," Paige teased.

Liz laughed and agreed. Picking up a gown Paige had tagged, she slipped it onto a matching satin hanger and adjusted the thin straps. "Considering you get first pick at everything, I'll just bet you have a ton of this stuff at home, don't you?"

"Some," she admitted, though she'd never received the dual enjoyment Liz boasted.

"Well, with your auburn hair and great figure, this one would look *fantastic* on you."

Paige eyed the calf-length nightgown Liz had retrieved from another shipment of lingerie. Emerald satin made up the skirt, but the bodice was sheer black lace, which matched the trim edging the thigh-high slit. "Uh, that one is a little risqué for me."

Liz rolled her eyes. "That's complete nonsense. If wearing this makes you feel good, then there's nothing indecent about it."

Paige noticed that Liz deliberately hung the gown on an empty rack next to the mirror, away from the other priced merchandise ready to be displayed in the boutique. Not wanting to make a fuss or elaborate on the issue, she made no comment. Later, she'd slip the gown back with the others.

They worked companionably for the next hour tagging the stock while Pam handled the front end of the store and the steady stream of Friday-afternoon customers. Paige instructed Liz where she wanted the merchandise, and the other woman scooped up an armful of clothes and headed out of the storeroom to hang the garments. While she was gone, Paige picked up the sexy, shimmery gown Liz had put aside, intending to put it back into the inventory.

Despite her remark about this piece of lingerie being too risqué for her, she gave in to temptation and lifted the vibrant gown to her figure, holding it snugly against her body with an arm across her waist. She imagined the rich, cool texture of the material sliding across her bare skin, the sensual rasp of black lace across her nipples…imagined feeling sexy, desirable, excited.

She drew a deep, shuddering breath. Lord knew she'd tried enticing Anthony with provocative lingerie, but he'd been so distracted and distant after their first year of marriage that all her attempts at seduction had failed to stir his interest. Those nights ended with her in bed alone, hurt and angry, while Anthony roamed restlessly through the house. When he had made love to her, it had been quick and emotionless, and she'd accommodated him out of duty, since Anthony gave little time and effort to her pleasure. And then he'd stopped touching her altogether. Tantalizing nightgowns were even less effective when divorce loomed on the horizon.

Her eyes fluttered closed, and she automatically thought about Josh, the way his hands caressed her body so lovingly, making her feel worshiped and incredibly voluptuous. The way his mouth, the stroke of his tongue, could ignite flash fires of need within her until it was all she could do not to go up in flames.

She'd never burned like that for Anthony, had never begged him to *touch her, kiss her* the way she'd shamelessly begged Josh. Just remembering how effortlessly she'd come undone for him made a delicious heat pool in her belly and brought a tingling flush to her skin.

"Very nice," a rich male voice murmured from behind her.

Startled out of her private thoughts, Paige's eyes flew open and she yanked the gown from her body. Turning around, she found Josh lounging casually in the doorway, male appreciation glimmering in his dark eyes. He looked entirely too sexy in khaki pants, a collared shirt, and a light sports jacket. And that beguiling grin tipping the corner of his mouth sent her pulse into a tailspin.

He pushed off the door frame and entered the room. "If you'd like to model it, I'd be a captive audience."

She'd just bet he would! "I don't think so," she said, hooking the gown back onto the rack.

He shrugged those broad shoulders of his, looking adorably mischievous. "Can't blame a guy for asking." His smile faded, dispelling the intimate moment. "So, how was your day?"

"Same as every other day this week." Her tone was sarcastic, but she couldn't hold back her resentment. "Long. Restrictive. No privacy."

"It can't be helped," he said sympathetically.

"No, I don't suppose it can be." Irritated for a number of reasons, she gathered the packing slips from that morning's shipment of clothes and put them in a neat pile on the counter.

"I've got something to show you," Josh said, smoothing over the awkward moment.

She fumbled with a paper clip, something to keep her hands busy. "Oh?"

"I put it in your office." He nodded his head in that direction. "C'mon and I'll show it to you."

Curious, she followed him out of the storeroom, her gaze automatically scanning the boutique for business. Liz was busy rearranging the lingerie section and doing a good job of it, and Pam was helping a customer at the register. Satisfied that all was well, she stepped into her office behind Josh.

He waved a hand at the portrait displayed on the wall where a watercolor painting had been. "So, what do you think?"

Heart hammering in her chest, Paige took a step closer to the painting of her wrapped in white fur, her neck now draped with that extravagant emerald-and-diamond necklace Anthony had stolen.

"I'm, well, uh… *Wow,*" was all she could manage to describe her astonishment. The likeness was striking, uncanny, entrancing…and certainly pretentious of her to hang in her office! But that was exactly what Carranza expected, Josh had told her.

Butterflies swarmed in her stomach, and she tore her gaze from that incredibly sensual picture to look at Josh. "So, now what do we do?"

Josh's smile was grim, foretelling the future. "We filter in the information about the portrait and the Ivanov necklace through our undercover officers working on the case, then we wait for Carranza to make his move."

6

THEY DIDN'T HAVE to wait long.

By Thursday of the following week Paige received a call from the broker she'd listed the boutique with. Matt Smythe informed her that a Victor Carranza was interested in purchasing the Wild Rose for his fiancée and wanted to meet with her personally. She knew it was all a ruse, a way for Carranza to get close to her and assess the situation. As Josh had instructed, she bought herself another twenty-four hours and set up an appointment to meet with Carranza Friday afternoon.

She thought she was ready for this moment. Josh had spent the weekend briefing her on various scenarios, and how to handle the carefully phrased questions that would no doubt arise in Carranza's quest for the necklace. She even had the security of a small, single-shot derringer Josh had borrowed from Liz for her to use in case of an extreme emergency. The weapon was tucked in the top drawer of her desk, and though a practice session last night at a shooting range had bolstered her confidence in wielding the derringer, the idea of having to resort to that kind of violence revolted her. Josh didn't think Carranza posed any danger to her at this point in the game, but they weren't taking any chances with her safety.

Everyone was in place for this afternoon's meeting. A bug had been placed in Paige's office so Josh and another detective could listen to their conversation from the surveillance van parked a few blocks away. Liz was armed beneath her fashionable crepe pantsuit and, as yet another precaution, a few undercover officers had been posted at the coffeehouse next to the Wild Rose.

"Your two o'clock appointment is here, Paige," Liz announced cheerfully as she entered the boutique's office, leading the way for the man following her. Liz's mouth held an amicable smile, but her eyes offered the reassurance and support Paige so desperately needed to get through this ordeal.

Pasting on a pleasant smile that concealed the anxiety coiling deep within her, she scooted her chair back from her rolltop desk and stood. "Thank you, Liz," she said, giving the other woman her cue to leave.

Liz hesitated briefly, her gaze darting toward the open door in what Paige could only construe as a subtle warning. The discreet, unspoken signal had Paige wishing she were a mind reader. Something in their plan had changed, but what?

Too soon, Liz exited the room. As they'd devised that morning, a decorative doorstop propped at the base of the door kept the office open, enabling the other woman to monitor the situation. Grateful for the modicum of safety, Paige forced herself to approach the ruthless man who'd had her husband murdered, a man who was out to claim a million-dollar necklace at any cost to the people involved.

He was nothing like the sinister, villainous criminal she'd envisioned. The man was tall, his tailored Italian suit fitting a physique slighter than the heavy, muscular build she had expected. His thick black hair was cut precisely, his eyes just as dark as those gleaming strands. His gaze, although sharp and assessing, radiated warmth, as did his benevolent smile. He appeared suave, obviously wealthy, and very...normal. Like any other businessman she'd ever met.

He extended a manicured hand toward her. "Paige Montgomery, I presume?" he queried, his voice deep and congenial.

"Yes." She didn't want to touch him, but to ignore his offered hand would be unacceptable. Shoring up her resolve, she politely slipped her hand into his. "It's nice to meet you, Mr. Carranza."

His eyes sparkled with the kind of persuasive charm designed to captivate an unsuspecting woman. Luckily, Paige knew enough to distrust this man.

"Considering we'll be doing business together, please call me Victor," he insisted.

The double meaning of his words "doing business together" sent a wave of apprehension sweeping through her. When she gently pulled her hand from his grasp, he didn't resist. "I do hope you find the boutique to your liking."

"I'm afraid I'm not the one you need to impress." He leaned close, winked, and added in a low, conspiratorial tone, "I brought the *critic* with me."

Before Paige had time to decipher that comment, a sleek, catlike woman stepped into the room, dressed in a racy-red, form-fitting halter dress that hugged her curves from breasts to thighs. Her endlessly long, tanned legs gave way to feet clad in red stiletto heels. A glittering ruby-and-diamond necklace, much too extravagant for daytime wear, encircled her neck, matching the teardrop earrings in her lobes and the jeweled bracelet adorning her wrist. In contrast, Paige felt like an old-fashioned matron in her conservative, double-breasted suit in a pale shade of sage.

This was the warning Liz had tried to give her, she realized. Even before Victor introduced her, Paige's stomach churned with the knowledge of who this woman was.

"Ah, there you are, pussycat," Victor said affectionately. "Come here and meet the owner of the Wild Rose." He waited until the gorgeous woman stood by his side before making the unnecessary introductions. "Paige, I'd like you to meet my fiancée, Bridget Piroux."

Paige desperately tried to keep her composure and act normal, which wasn't an easy feat considering she was meeting the woman with whom her husband had had an illicit, deadly affair. Curiously, she'd thought that when this moment came she'd experience jealousy or some other violent emotion, but all she felt was renewed anger at Anthony's duplicity. This woman was proof that her marriage to Anthony had been a sham based on lies and deceit—if that hadn't been evident before, it was now.

She smiled amicably, but didn't offer her hand. "It's nice to meet you."

The other woman gave her head a haughty shake, and her long sable hair rippled down her back in a silky cascade. Dark, exotic green eyes that tipped up at the corners scrutinized Paige from head to toe. Full lips, painted the same shocking red as her dress curled into a smug smile. "Ummm, a pleasure," she purred.

"So, what do you think of the place, pussycat?"

Bridget hooked an arm through Victor's, pressing so close her breasts quivered and threatened to spill from her low-cut bodice. "Darling, the boutique is absolutely charming!" she gushed, playing the pampered fiancée to the hilt. "The shop is classy and the outfits are more stylish than I'd expected. Why, it would be like having one great big closet full of clothes!"

Under different circumstances, Paige would have found the other woman's fatuousness amusing, but there was a shrewd intelligence in her eyes that belied her dim-witted, spoiled routine.

Victor caught the hand that had slipped intimately beneath his suit jacket and brought it back into sight. "How long do you think it will hold your attention before you grow bored with it?"

Laughing throatily, she trailed a long, crimson nail along the front of his shirt. "Does it really matter, as long as it keeps me busy during the day while you're working?"

"No, I suppose it doesn't." He sighed and looked back at Paige with a shrug that said he was helpless to resist this woman's wishes. "I guess we'll be discussing numbers."

Paige prayed her surprise didn't reflect on her face. She honestly hadn't believed his supposed interest in the boutique would go beyond a preliminary inquiry. And what perplexed her even more was that, so far, neither one of them had glanced at the picture on the wall. Wasn't that their *real* purpose for being here?

"All right," Paige said, playing along with the ruse. She waved a hand toward the pair of tweed chairs and end table that made up a small sitting area next to her desk. "Please, sit down and we'll discuss my price and terms."

Victor took one of the chairs, but Bridget strolled to the opposite side of the office from where the portrait hung. She stopped at a bookcase filled with catalogs, specialty books and other business periodicals. Retrieving a thick book of fashion designs, she casually flipped through the pages.

"I'm afraid she doesn't care for the dealing part of business, and leaves the final decision in my hands," Carranza said, explaining Bridget's disinterest.

More likely she wants to case the joint, Paige thought, but feigned indifference. "I understand."

Opening the button on his suit jacket, he reclined back in his chair. "First, I'd like to ask why you're selling the boutique."

The personal question threw her, though she managed to sustain an outward calm. "Excuse me?"

"I'm sorry, I didn't mean to be so blunt." He smiled his apology. "But what I'd like to know is if the Wild Rose is financially secure."

"It turns a decent profit. In fact, it's doing extremely well." Not sure where this conversation was heading, but wanting to maintain a businesslike air, she offered, "I can have my accountant send you a financial statement if you'd like."

"If the boutique is solvent, why would you let it go?" he asked, as if he hadn't heard her last remark or was ignoring it for more consequential information. "Is there something we should know about, a reason why you might be, well, *unloading* the shop…"

Paige was beginning to find this conversation entirely too bizarre, as if Carranza really *did* have an interest in the boutique, which was ridiculous. These pragmatic questions weren't what she'd anticipated, and her honest answer to his question—that she was severing all ties to Miami and opting for solitude and simplicity—weren't appropriate in this situation.

Think pretentious and pampered, Paige. That's what they expect from you. "Oh, no, it's nothing like that," she said, punctuating her remark with light, frivolous laughter. "The boutique is a responsibility I no longer want. I'm recently widowed, and I've been thinking of doing some traveling." *Straight to Connecticut.*

"Alone?" His smile was affable, his tone conversational, but there was something in the depths of his gaze that made her feel anxious—as if he was subtly prying for intimate answers that had nothing to do with the sale of the boutique and more to do with the ostentatious woman she was supposed to be.

Out of the corner of her eye she noticed Bridget watching her, waiting for her response, her fingers stroking the dazzling ruby-and-diamond necklace Paige highly suspected had been smuggled through Carranza's organization.

Paige's face warmed, and she hoped they'd both mistake the flush for embarrassment and not the uneasiness it was. "Well, no, not exactly," she lied.

Bracing his arms on the side of the chair, the suave man steepled his fingers in front of him and regarded her over the tips. "A male companion, then?" he asked curiously.

His audacity astounded her. She knew she was supposed to be accommodating, but she was beginning to feel interrogated, and annoyed. "Mr. Carranza," she said firmly, attempting to steer their conversation back to business. "I don't know what my traveling plans have to do with your interest in the boutique...."

He held up a hand and appeared apologetic. "I'm sorry. I'm afraid I tend to let my curiosity get the best of me at times. You're a lovely woman, and I just naturally assumed you'd have an escort."

Belatedly, Paige realized the reason for his casual

probing. They'd heard about Josh being her lover and wanted to confirm the report they'd been given.

He shrugged, as if dismissing the entire verbal exchange. "Back to business, then. What are you asking for the boutique?"

She quoted him the price she'd estimated the Wild Rose was worth, and spent the next fifteen minutes discussing her terms for the sale, treating him as she would any other potential buyer. He digested the information she fed him, and asked all the appropriate questions of a prospective investor. During that time Bridget continued her slow perusal of the office, and Liz passed the door with an armload of clothes and glanced surreptitiously inside, offering Paige a measure of comfort and security, though she felt no direct threat from Carranza.

When there was nothing left to discuss but an offer, Carranza stood and rebuttoned his suit jacket. "Before making any final decisions, I'd like to discuss the purchase with my investment broker."

This couldn't be the end of his visit, she thought, finding his strategy disconcerting and unnerving. Following his lead, she retrieved a business card from her desk and handed it to him. "Feel free to give me a call if you or your broker have any other questions."

"Oh, I'm certain you'll be hearing back from me shortly." His smile held a deeper connotation than his simple words.

"Darling, would you take a look at this picture!" Bridget exclaimed, capturing their attention.

Paige and Victor turned at the same moment to find the other woman in front of the portrait hanging on the wall, her eyes alight with excitement and intense purpose.

Finally, Paige thought, relief and nervousness colliding.

Victor casually strolled to where Bridget stood. Hands thrust into the front pockets of his slacks, he considered the sensual portrait of Paige wrapped in white fur, her cleavage a perfect setting for the Ivanov necklace. "Umm, the picture *is* quite exquisite," he said, with a slow, appreciative grin that made Paige's skin crawl.

Bridget's eyes narrowed in the pretense of being a slighted lover. "I want this necklace to complete my collection," she said haughtily.

He stroked his chin with his fingers, as if contemplating her demand. "Pussycat," he began in a tone meant to placate, "you can't have everything you want."

Her expression turned sullen. "I have everything but emeralds, and you told me when I found something I liked you would buy it for me, regardless of the cost. This is the necklace I want."

Carranza glanced at Paige, looking appropriately exasperated by his fiancée's behavior—but not enough to deny her. "Do you mind if I ask where you bought the necklace?"

Paige's heart pounded so hard, she feared he'd be able to see it thumping beneath her prim suit. Gradually moving closer to where they both stood, she forced herself to concentrate on the various responses she and Josh had rehearsed. *Drop subtle clues,* he'd told her.

"Oh, I didn't buy it," she said, amazed to find her voice so steady when her insides were quaking. "After my husband died a few months ago I found the necklace stashed in a safe I have at home. Most likely it was a gift he never had the chance to give me."

"How much do you want for it?" Bridget asked imperiously.

Paige met her ruthless stare, wondering what Anthony had seen in the other woman that he'd risked his life for. Excitement? Danger? "I'm sorry, it's not for sale."

The other woman's gaze turned frosty, chilling Paige to the bone. "*Everything* has a price, and Victor will gladly pay yours."

"Now, Pussycat," Carranza began, patting her arm consolingly. "If it's not for sale—"

"*I want it,*" she stated angrily, and in a swirl of red left the office.

Paige drew a steady breath, a little shaken by the dark, merciless glint she'd seen in Bridget's gaze. She knew her tantrum had been a performance, but her rancor had seemed so real....

After a moment, Victor cast Paige a contrite look, as if to say his fiancée's petulance was a common occurrence he'd grown used to. "I'm afraid when she sets her mind to something she doesn't let up until she gets it. Maybe you could reconsider selling the necklace?"

Paige's insides were clenching, churning. She struggled to keep up her end of the farce, hating every minute of it. "I have to confess that I suspect the necklace is a fake, and not nearly as valuable as your fiancée might believe."

"Really?" His brows rose in surprise. "You had it appraised?"

She shook her head. "No, but I know my husband couldn't have afforded a necklace like that if the jewels were authentic."

"Hmmm." He scrutinized the portrait once more. "Would you be opposed to having the necklace looked at by my appraiser? I'd be willing to offer market value, plus thirty percent, fake or no."

She'd bet odds that his appraiser would conclude that the jewels were synthetic, and not worth more than a couple of hundred dollars—an uncomplicated, easy transaction for a million-dollar necklace. No murder, no mayhem, no more encounters with *the witch*. She was tempted, but knew that simple route wasn't an option.

Play hard to get. Josh's words echoed in her mind. "That's very generous of you, but I really don't think—"

"Trust me, buying this necklace, at any cost, will save me a lot of grief where Bridget is concerned." He smiled persuasively. "Tell you what. I'm having a dinner party next Saturday at my estate in the Keys. Why don't you join us? I have a guest cottage you're welcome to use for the weekend."

"Oh, I couldn't possibly." Dread twisted within her when she thought of staying at this man's estate, alone, at his complete mercy. She grasped for an excuse to refuse his offer. "I'm seeing someone, and I don't think he'd like me attending a party without him."

"By all means, bring him along," he suggested generously. "My appraiser will be there. Bring the necklace, I'll have him look at it, and we can make a deal that will benefit both of us." He winked at her, and without giving her time to refuse said, "I'll be in touch to give you directions to my estate."

She watched him leave her office, heard his voice mingling with Bridget's, then the tinkle of the boutique's door chime as they left the Wild Rose. Dimly, she realized that he'd left no business card, no phone number, or any other way to contact him. She was like a spider caught in his web—relinquishing the Ivanov necklace would be her only means of escape.

She stood there, alone in the office, her body trembling in a series of tiny aftershocks that kicked up her adrenaline. Everything had gone as planned. They were going to be on Carranza's turf, just as Lieutenant Reynolds wanted. Except she had no desire to display that necklace, or be a part of such a potentially deadly scheme—no matter how much protection Josh promised her.

She had no choice. That realization brought on a wave of anger so fierce, it heated her blood and made her tense enough to snap at Liz when she slipped into the office and asked if she was okay.

Hell, no, she wasn't okay! She had absolutely no control over the situation, or her life at the moment, and she resented every bit of it—from Anthony's deceit, to Carranza's ruthlessness, to being forced into a dangerous situation that put her life at risk. Liz attempted to reason with her, but she was far from feeling rational. Not when her entire future looked shaky at best.

Within ten minutes of Carranza's departure, Josh arrived at the boutique, no doubt having heard her snapping at Liz through the van's surveillance system. The door Liz had shut to give them privacy swung open without a knock and Josh strode inside, his expression fierce and focused on Paige.

"Give us a few minutes alone, Liz," he ordered without looking at the other woman.

"Sure." Relief laced Liz's voice. Slipping out of the room before the fireworks started, she closed the door behind her.

Josh came up to Paige and rested his hands gently on her shoulders. "You did just fine, sweetheart," he said, his thumbs stroking along her neck in an attempt to relax her.

"I did just fine?" Her voice was shrill. She was ready for a fight, itching to vent the turbulent emotions building within her. "My God, Josh, I came face-to-face with the woman Anthony had an affair with, and the man who had him murdered!" There was no need to explain any of the conversation she'd had with Carranza—he'd heard every word from the surveillance van. "What's to stop him from killing me, too?"

Something dark and dangerous flashed in his eyes, then was gone. "All he wants is the necklace, which we're going to make sure he confiscates so we can prosecute him. We're right where we want to be."

"*You're* right where *you* want to be, you mean." Finding his touch much too distracting, she stepped away from him. Her nerves remained coiled tight. "Isn't there some other way to lure Carranza?"

"No." Though his gaze held understanding, his inflexible tone cut off any further objections. "He knows you have the necklace and, judging by the conversation we heard, he intends to confiscate it—with or without your cooperation. *I* prefer we cooperate, which means accepting his dinner invitation."

She glared at him for long moments, wanting to argue, wanting to refuse. He stared back unflinchingly, unwilling to compromise. Protesting would be a waste of breath, she knew.

"Fine," she said flatly, turning away from him and going to her desk. Gathering files, she stuffed them into her briefcase, her movements brusque. "Now, if you don't mind, it's been a long day and I'd like you to take me home."

THE MOMENT Josh parked the car in the garage, he knew something was wrong. He sensed trouble on a gut level, but there was evidence as well to back up his intuition.

He turned to Paige as she unsnapped her seat belt and grabbed her arm before she could open her door. "I want you to stay in the car, keep the engine running, and lock the doors," he said in as neutral a tone of voice as he could manage, so he didn't unnecessarily frighten her. "And move over to the driver's side once I'm out."

Apprehension touched her tired features. "Josh, what's wrong?"

"The house alarm. It's been disengaged." As he'd expected, she automatically glanced at the security keypad next to the door to confirm that the red light was out, verification the alarm had been tampered with in some way. "Stay put. I'm going inside to check things out."

"Josh, no," she said, panic tingeing her voice.

"I'll be fine," he reassured her. "But if you see anyone you don't recognize I want you to leave, then call the police on the cell phone."

Before she could object, he slid out of the Volvo, made sure she followed his instructions, then withdrew his gun from his shoulder holster and soundlessly made his way inside the house. The interior was shadowed with twilight, the structure eerily quiet—there was nothing to indicate an intruder lurked within the dwelling.

He flipped a light switch on the wall in the living room and swore vibrantly. The house had been ransacked. Couches were overturned, the matching cushions and throw pillows slashed open, the white fiber filling spilling out onto the floor. Cabinets and drawers had been rummaged through, their contents strewn haphazardly around the room. Pictures had been ripped off the walls, lamps had been smashed, and anything not bolted down had been upended.

Every room in the house was the same—pillaged and vandalized in someone's quest to locate the Ivanov necklace. Of that, Josh was certain. Carranza knew Paige had the piece of jewelry, and had obviously sent his men to find it. Except it wasn't here, as they'd no doubt discovered.

Knowing there was no possible way they could stay here tonight, he grabbed his duffel bag from Paige's ravaged room, tossed in his personal things and her toiletries, and decided they'd stay at a hotel until the place was secured, dusted for fingerprints, and cleaned up.

His head shot up and his entire body tensed when he heard a noise from the other room. Christ, were the thugs still here? Then a low, choking noise followed—a sound that lifted the hairs at the back of his neck and turned him stone-cold.

He thought of Paige, sitting alone in the car. He thought of the possibility of one of Carranza's men harming her, and knew they'd be dead before they realized he'd put a bullet through their heart.

Adrenaline and rage rushed through his veins as he moved silently toward the front rooms. Another indiscernible sound reached him. He rounded the last corner, his finger tight on the trigger, gun aimed and steady…right at Paige's heart.

7

"JESUS, PAIGE, what in the *hell* possessed you to do something so incredibly stupid?" Josh's voice was a low roar in the small motel room he'd secured for them for the night. "I could have killed you!"

Paige glared at him, but didn't move from where she stood by the closed, locked and chained motel room door. The raw energy and tension radiating off Josh was nearly tangible, and though she wasn't the least bit intimidated by his grim expression or dark tone of voice, she knew better than to get near the eye of a hurricane.

Admittedly, she'd been horrified and shaken by what she'd witnessed back at her house, not to mention terrified by the way Josh had snuck up on her and confronted her with his drawn gun. Now that her shock had had time to ebb, she felt angry, completely violated, and in no mood for one of Josh's lectures.

After that frightening ordeal in her living room over half an hour ago, Josh had promptly issued a vile string of curses, holstered his gun, and then, with a tenacious grip on her arm, had ushered her out of the house and back into the car. She'd complied with no argument; the vandalism and wreckage within her house had rendered her speechless.

He'd restrained his fury during the call he'd immediately placed to Lieutenant Reynolds on his cell phone to report the break-in and to let his senior officer know where they'd be staying for the night. He'd fumed the short distance to the motel, his jaw clenched hard, his entire body rigid. He'd even managed to control his temper when he'd arranged a room for them and she'd primly requested two double beds.

But now, he seemed hell-bent on releasing that pent-up wrath, and there was nothing she could do to escape the storm except ride it out.

"I asked you to wait in the car," Josh went on furiously, pacing agitatedly on the strip of worn, olive-green carpeting between the foot of the beds and the scarred dresser against the nearest wall. "Why couldn't you obey that simple request?"

Paige bristled at his demand, and knew she had two options at this point—let the hysteria she'd so far managed to keep at bay overcome her and fall apart, or fight back. Because she knew the former would do her absolutely no good, she reached deep for resources she was just beginning to tap into—strength, resistance and fortitude—and leveled all three at Josh.

Her chin rose up a few notches. "I went into the house because it seemed like you were taking forever and I was worried about you." At the time, she'd been scared of being alone and that something awful would happen to Josh. She didn't claim her actions had been smart, but they'd been instinctive, driven by helpless fears and vulnerable emotions.

"Worried about me?" His voice hit an incredulous pitch, and he abruptly stopped his edgy, back-and-forth stride. "For crying out loud, Paige, I'm the one with the weapon and training, not you! What would you have done if one of Carranza's men had attacked you while you were in the house?"

She'd thought of that—when Josh had slipped soundlessly into the living room and trained his gun at her, prepared to shoot what he'd believed was an intruder. In that moment, staring down the barrel of his pistol, her heart had stopped, and she'd experienced a sickening sense of déjà vu.

Swallowing the acrid taste in her mouth, along with the equally bitter memories threatening to engulf her, she offered him the only answer—as insubstantial as it was—that came to mind. "Liz taught me some self-defense maneuvers."

His bark of laughter was harsh and insensitive. "Trust me, sweetheart, no self-defense tactic would have stood a chance against one of Carranza's men. You might have been able to disable him for a few seconds to gain some time, but you wouldn't have gotten very far before he caught up to you." A ruthless glint entered his eyes. "And you don't even want to think about what he'd do to you when he found you again. He'd be merciless."

Josh's brutal words, combined with his callous tone and flinty expression, sent an ominous chill slithering down her spine. He was trying to scare her into submission, she knew, but everything he'd just told her had already invaded her thoughts at one time or another the past few weeks. "There's nothing to stop his men from attacking me anytime, anywhere."

"Trust me, *I'd* stop them." Planting his hands on his hips, he fixed his golden-brown gaze on her. "But you make it extremely difficult for me to keep you safe when you blatantly ignore my orders. I give them to you for a specific reason, Paige, not to be controlling or manipulative."

She didn't miss the insinuation in his carefully chosen words. He'd all but tacked *like Anthony* on to the end of his sentence.

"Like tonight," he continued, slicing a hand through the air to emphasize his point. "I asked you to wait in the car, a simple request so I'd know where you were and so you'd have half a chance of getting out alive if something went wrong. And what do you do? You leave the safety of the car, come into the house, and nearly get yourself killed!" His temper built to a new crescendo, and he impaled her with his sharp gaze. "How can I do my job and protect you when you won't let me?"

Paige valiantly tried to keep a tether on her temper, tried desperately to remain calm and rational, but felt the restraint on her emotions slipping. The tension that had been building all day—knotting her nerves, twisting her insides, playing havoc with her sanity—finally reached a pinnacle. The intense pressure within her demanded freedom, and she embraced the flood of adrenaline that finally gave her the impetus to release the stress.

"This is *my* life that has been turned upside down and inside out. How do you think that makes *me* feel?" He looked caught off balance by her unexpected barrage, and she didn't wait for him to regain his equilibrium. "I haven't had a moment's privacy in weeks, or a decent night's rest since this all began. I've come face-to-face with my husband's lover *and* his killer, who wants a necklace from me that I'd gladly *give* to him if I could, just to put an end to this nightmare. My house has been ransacked for something I don't even have, what little I cherish has been destroyed, and I feel violated by the intrusion into my home, my *life*."

While the strain, grief and distress of the past few

weeks poured out of her, she advanced on him, until they stood less than two feet apart. Her heart thumped madly, and her hands clenched into tight fists at her sides. "And, to top off everything, for the second time in my life, I've had the threat of a gun aimed at me, and I resent every bit of it!"

The anger hardening his features faded, and his expression went carefully blank. "What did you just say?" he asked in a low tone of voice.

Had he ignored her entire tirade? Impatience surged through her, and she jabbed a pointed finger in his firmly muscled chest, enunciating her words so there was no way he could misunderstand her. "I said, *I resent every bit of it!*"

He shook his head, his brows slanting into a frown. "I heard that part, loud and clear." The only illumination in the room came from the lamp on the nightstand between the beds. The dim light cast shadows over his face, making him appear dark and dangerous. "I'm talking about the part about the gun."

She was suddenly too close, she thought. Especially since she could feel the heat vibrating off his body. Could hear the slow, deep breaths he took. Could see the sharp, assessing look in his eyes as they stared into hers, searching for a response.

Realizing she'd admitted more than she'd meant to, and he meant to pursue an issue she had no desire to discuss, she attempted to move away from him, to the small table with two chairs located in the corner of the room.

He grabbed her upper arm before she could execute that plan. The authority in his grip was unrelenting, but not bruising. "Dammit, Paige," he growled angrily. "You brought it up, so I expect an answer!"

She tugged gently on her arm, and he let it go, though she knew there was no way he'd let her avoid the discussion. Wearily, she sat down on the edge of the bed.

Releasing a shuddering breath, she prepared herself to relive the final hours she'd shared with Anthony. "The last night Anthony spent at home he was on edge. The entire night he roamed restlessly through the house, double-checking the locks on the doors and windows, and making sure the alarm was on." She glanced up at Josh, her lips twisting into a mocking smile. "At least now I understand why he was acting so strange."

Josh rested his backside against the dresser and crossed his arms over his chest. "Go on."

"When I found him in the morning he was sleeping upright on the couch, with his gun in his lap. When I tried to wake him, he jumped up and leveled the gun at my chest. His eyes were crazed, and I just stood there, waiting for him to pull the trigger." She'd thought the memory would hurt, cause her emotional pain, but she only felt empty inside. "And in that moment I realized that my husband was a complete stranger. I didn't know him at all."

Josh said nothing, but then words were unnecessary when his appalled expression clearly communicated his feelings.

She touched her tongue to her dry lips and continued. "Never once did he apologize for nearly killing me, *his wife*, but instead screamed at me to never sneak up on him again. That's when I knew it was over between us. Completely over."

"And that's when you finally decided to file for divorce," he guessed.

"Yeah." Feeling that awful tension building within her again, brewed out of bitterness, she stood and moved around the small, stuffy room. "I'd first asked him for a divorce about six months before this incident, and he said no," she told him, revealing more personal issues Josh had no knowledge of.

"I can't imagine Anthony's refusal would stop you from doing anything you wanted to after the first year of marriage you experienced," Josh said, a wry note to his voice. "What made you stay?"

She was still wearing the sage suit she'd worn to work that day, and the lined jacket was beginning to feel hot and suffocating. Since there was little chance of them leaving for the night, she shrugged out of the jacket, revealing a cream silk camisole. "I thought maybe if he knew I had no qualms about leaving him, things would change between us," she admitted, realizing now just how naive she'd been about the possibility of Anthony taking an active role in their marriage. The man had been too selfish to offer what she'd ultimately needed from him. Love, and maybe a little of his time and attention. And she'd wanted things he'd had no intention of giving her, like children, and being a family. "If anything, our marriage got worse. Shortly after that confrontation, I found evidence of an affair, which of course he denied." Folding the coat, she laid it neatly over one of the chairs. "The stress and tension between us accumulated until I just couldn't take it anymore. The incident with the gun was the final straw."

He swore and scrubbed a hand along his jaw.

She shrugged, having had many months to get accustomed to the truth. One of the biggest clues of his infidelity had been that he hadn't made love to her, or even touched her, in so much longer than was normal for a married couple.

Slipping her shoes off her aching feet, she left them by the side of the bed farthest from the door. "I thought that last morning together would be the end of all the heartache and misery, but it seems it was just the beginning."

"Ah, Paige…" He pushed off the dresser and started toward her, compassion glimmering in his gaze.

"Don't." She held up a hand to ward him off, not wanting his tenderness, pity or the apology she knew was hovering on his lips. And there was also the problem of her being trapped in between two beds and his solid body.

He stopped, confusion transforming his features. "Don't what?"

"Don't you *dare* apologize, because right now it means nothing when my life is hanging somewhere between survival and hell." The guilt that flashed in his eyes confirmed that she'd read him correctly. "I don't want this, but I'm forced into it because of Anthony. I'm tired of always looking over my shoulder, and I'm tired of people telling me what to do."

He took a step toward her, thought better of the idea when she glared at him, and halted again. "Paige—"

"I know I have no choice in the matter," she recited, another educated guess at what he would have said. "That none of this will end until this case is closed and over, but that doesn't make me any less angry. I had enough of this sort of upheaval when I was married to Anthony, this kind of uncertainty and fear. I thought it ended when he died, that I could get on with my life and have a semblance of normalcy. Now, everything is falling apart, and there isn't a damn thing I can do about it." Her voice caught, faltered, and she struggled to maintain her composure. "I don't even have a house to live in anymore."

"The detectives on the case will need a few days to search for evidence, which I'm doubtful they'll find." His mouth thinned in resignation. "The house should be cleaned up and back in order shortly after that. You could probably be back in by the end of next week."

Her brows rose. "And you think I actually *want* to go back there, after what happened tonight?" Her tone of voice said he was crazy for making such a suggestion. "I can't go back, because nothing will ever be the same again. It was bad enough when you discovered the hidden safe, but now someone has actually invaded my home, pawed through my possessions, and tainted everything in that house."

"I know," he said quietly, as if he understood, but didn't quite know what to do to ease her uncertainties.

She made it easy on him. "Since I can't bring myself to spend another night in that house, I'll be hiring someone next week to pack up all my belongings except for the necessities, and have everything shipped to my sister's place. Once this is over, I'm leaving, Josh. Once you slap handcuffs on Carranza, I'll be on the first flight back to Connecticut."

His gaze flickered over her face, so tender, so cherishing. "I'd really like you to rethink your plans."

He all but wore his heart on his sleeve, and that open display of emotion was nearly her undoing. She was horrified to feel a rush of hot tears burning the back of her eyes and tightening her throat. She was incapable of speaking, which was probably for the best because she didn't want to hurt him any more with her answer, and there was no way she would ever offer him false hopes or promises for a future together. Their situation was hopeless, for so many reasons...and everything tied into Anthony.

Anthony had brought them together. And Anthony would tear them apart.

Needing to be alone before she finally gave in to the emotional release hovering just beyond the superficial self-control she'd managed to maintain all day, she escaped to the only place that afforded her any privacy: the bathroom.

SITTING ON his rumpled, unmade bed across from Paige's, Josh watched her sleep during the early, shadowed hours of morning, unable to remember the last time he'd seen her so peaceful. She looked breathtakingly beautiful with her features softened, and her silky auburn hair tousled around her face. Her relaxed mouth even curved ever-so-slightly into a sweet, serene smile. It was all an illusion, he knew, because as soon as she woke up, reality would intrude and steal away the tranquility touching her expression.

But until then, he enjoyed the quiet simplicity of just looking at her and letting his imagination indulge in some pleasant, sensual thoughts. His gaze roamed slowly down the length of her as she lay on her side, her hands tucked beneath her pillow. The motel's outdated air-conditioning hadn't sputtered out enough cool air to make the clanking, chugging sound worth a sleepless night, so they'd opted to leave the unit off. As a result, the room was warm, and Paige had kicked off her covers.

Since he hadn't grabbed any clothing for her at the house, last night he'd offered her one of his T-shirts to sleep in, which she filled out incredibly well. The soft cotton molded to her full breasts, and he could see the rosy crests through the white material. He imagined brushing his fingers over the tips, teasing them to hardness, then soothing that ache with the slippery wetness of his tongue, the heated depths of his mouth....

She sighed softly through parted lips, and rolled to her back. The full swell of her breasts, crowned with tight, beaded nipples, pushed enticingly against the shirt she wore. His mouth watered, his body quickened, and his blood heated and spread low in his belly, then lower still, until it gathered in his loins.

The hem was bunched around her hips, affording him an intimate view of white, silky panties, and sleek, long legs. In his mind, he pictured sliding his hands along the back of her calves, stroking the sensitive spot he'd discovered behind her knee the night they'd made love, too long ago. Envisioned skimming his fingers up her smooth thighs, using his palms and the stroke of his tongue to cajole them to part, then pressing his mouth to the silk covering that intimate, feminine part of her to taste her passion and bring her to the brink of desire. And then, once she'd found that first exquisite release, he'd strip away that flimsy barrier, wrap her thighs tight around his hips, and ease deep, deep inside her, until she climaxed again and took him with her....

A low moan purred in her throat—as if his thoughts had somehow slipped into her mind—and her legs shifted, rubbing sensually, restlessly together. Beneath the zipper of his jeans he grew hard, uncomfortably so. Her breathing deepened, her chest rising and falling as heavily, as rapidly, as his own.

Christ. Deciding to end the physical torment he'd inflicted upon himself, with no relief in sight, he flopped back onto the mattress and squeezed his eyes shut, attempting to focus his mind on anything except losing himself in the lush warmth of Paige's body, anything but the way his thoughts could seemingly become a part of her own....

Her response to him, even in sleep, shouldn't have surprised him. They'd always shared a special connection, which they'd blanketed in a nice, cozy friendship because of her marriage to Anthony. But that subliminal bond had always been there, even if she'd been physically off-limits. Invisible lines had been drawn from the moment Anthony had laid eyes on her and staked a claim—Josh had been there that fateful night and clearly remembered the events that had irrevocably changed Paige's life.

She'd come to Miami with her sister, Valerie, for a weeklong summer vacation, intending to soak up the sun on the beach during the day, and enjoy the local nightlife in the evenings. When he'd first spotted Paige from across the crowded, popular Miami nightclub where Anthony had coerced him into meeting him, the first thing that had caught Josh's attention was her natural beauty. She stood out from the rest of the heavily made-up women wearing tight, clingy clothes meant to tempt and entice the men in the bar. Such brazen women were more Anthony's style and had never appealed to Josh, which made Paige's fresh face and her calf-length, sarong-style dress all the more attractive to him.

As he'd surreptitiously watched her from the bar while shooting the breeze with Anthony and nursing a beer, he noticed other things that appealed to him: her vibrance, her quick smiles and lilting laughter, and those guileless green eyes that seemed so clear and bottomless.

Unfortunately, Paige had snared Anthony's attention

as well, though Josh never would have guessed how deeply Anthony's interest had run or his purpose for pursuing her. At the time, he'd suspected Anthony's competitive nature had been part of the initial chase— Paige would never know that Josh had slid off his bar stool to approach her first, only to have Anthony beat him to the punch. Before both of Josh's feet could hit the floor, Anthony had purchased a bottle of the wine Paige had been drinking and was heading across the crowded room to deliver it to her personally.

Josh didn't bother to rise to Anthony's silent challenge. He'd seen Anthony work his charm on enough women to know that he didn't stand a chance. So he'd watched his friend weave his magic and seduce the unsuspecting woman—all the while hoping Anthony's interest in Paige would eventually wane, as it had with all the other women he dated.

This time was different. This time, Anthony had underlying motivations even Josh would never have imagined possible. Three months later, Anthony had moved Paige from Connecticut and married her in a lavish ceremony with over three hundred guests attending. Within a year of that joyous occasion, Anthony's obsession with Paige finally became clear. Anthony hadn't wanted a wife, but an asset, someone wholesome and sweet to complete his warped perception of "having it all." Ambition. Power. Wealth. And a beautiful, genteel wife on his arm when the need arose.

Anthony's interest *had* diminished, just as it always did, just as Josh thought it would, leaving Paige disillusioned, confused and struggling to understand what had gone wrong. And the only thing he could do was offer her friendship and support, when he wanted to give her so much more.

Josh opened his eyes and stared at the water-stained ceiling, wondering, not for the first time, how differently things would have turned out if he'd accepted Anthony's challenge that night at the club and pursued Paige as well. Certainly falling in love with her was a given, considering how his feelings for her had evolved. And there was no doubt he would have married her. Likely, by now, they would have had at least one baby, maybe two....

His stomach twisted with so many regrets. He still wanted those things with her, but knew he didn't stand much of a chance when it came to competing with the bitter memories instilled by Anthony's egotistical aspirations.

He thought about the possibility of her being pregnant with his child, but as much as the idea of having a baby with Paige appealed to him, that particular wish was a selfish one on his part. A child would give him a stronger tie to Paige, a bond that would last forever, yet he knew she might resent being thrust into a relationship with him—one she clearly didn't want.

Feeling restless, and frustrated at his inability to control the future, he left the bed and went to the only window in the room, pushing aside the heavy drapes a few inches. The first fringes of dawn were spreading across the sky, promising a warm, sunny Saturday. He hated to waste such a perfect day inside this awful motel room or at the boutique. And he knew without a doubt Paige wasn't mentally ready to return to the beach house.

The past few weeks had been hell for Paige, and he wanted to offer her a small slice of heaven to offset the burdens she'd had to bear. He wanted to see the luster in her eyes again, wanted to hear her laughter, and would sell his soul to see one of her genuine, dazzling smiles.

He needed that. So did she. And he was confident a quick, weekend getaway would restore both of their spirits and put them in a better frame of mind for what lay ahead. Maybe his idea might work to his favor, too, and prove to Paige that marriage to a cop wasn't always heartache.

Spying a small doughnut shop across the street, he smiled, an idea forming. He needed to contact Reynolds, apprise him of his plans and get his approval. Since he didn't want to use the phone in the room and possibly wake Paige when she needed the rest, he figured he could call Reynolds on his cell phone as he walked the short distance to get him and Paige breakfast—and still keep an eye on their motel room.

Since he'd been unable to sleep, he'd showered and changed into jeans and a collared knit shirt earlier. Securing his Beretta into his holster, he put on his lightweight sports coat and slipped quietly from the room, making sure the door was locked behind him.

When he returned ten minutes later, Paige was curled up on her side facing the door, but still asleep. Now that his plans were in motion, and he had Reynolds's wholehearted consent, he was anxious for them to be on their way.

Setting the foam cup of freshly brewed coffee on the nightstand in between the two beds, along with a warm, fragrant cinnamon-streusel muffin, he hunkered down in front of Paige and gently blew the scented curls of steam her way.

She drew a deep breath, and her nostrils flared.

Grinning, he sent another aromatic draft her way.

She moaned, the sound low and appreciative.

One more time, and her eyes fluttered open, unfocused, but beautiful nonetheless.

"Good morning, sleepyhead," he murmured.

"It was, until you woke me up," she groused. Then a slow smile curved her mouth and she stretched languidly, making his body quicken. "I was having a wonderful dream."

He chuckled warmly, remembering his earlier erotic thoughts. "Was I in it?" he dared to ask.

A flush deepened the rosy hue of her complexion. "Maybe." Her voice held husky nuances, whether a residual of sleep or arousal, he wasn't sure.

She might have been fuming mad at him last night and gone to bed upset, but this morning there was no trace of bitterness. Admittedly, her anger never lasted long with him. They argued and moved on. She didn't hold grudges like some women, didn't punish by allowing her animosity to develop into a cold attitude that lasted for days.

He figured her tirade had been a long-overdue release, and a therapeutic one at that. A person could only take so much pressure before they blew, and he suspected yesterday's events had pushed Paige to her limit. This morning, however, she appeared refreshed and receptive, though he didn't doubt for a moment that the case wasn't far from her mind.

Her light mood encouraged him, and he took advantage of it. "Maybe I could persuade you to forgive me for interrupting such a great dream." Standing, he readjusted her pillows against the headboard and motioned for her to sit up, which she did, dragging the sheet with her to cover up her bare legs. He found her sudden bout of modesty endearing, especially since he'd already indulged in eyeing every inch of her. "I went across the street and got us coffee and fresh-baked muffins."

She pushed her hair out of her face and considered his bribe. A teasing gleam brightened her green eyes, giving him a glimpse of the fun-loving Paige he'd met three years ago. "You'd take advantage of a woman's weaknesses that way?"

Sitting on the edge of the bed next to her hip, he handed her one of the cups of coffee. "Just yours," he admitted, enjoying their flirtatious banter. His hopes for a relaxing, pleasant weekend soared.

She wrapped her fingers around the warmth and took a sip of the fragrant brew. "Umm..." She closed her eyes briefly, savoring the rich flavor. "This is wonderful."

He smiled at her blissful expression. "So is the muffin." He broke off a piece of the spiced cake topped with sweet, crunchy streusel and held it to her lips. "Try a bite."

She hesitated, the intimacy of the situation swirling between them. Then, as if accepting his unspoken challenge, she allowed him to feed her the muffin. He purposely touched his fingers to her lips, dragged his thumb along the corner of her mouth to catch a crumb. Awareness flared in her eyes, coiled deep in his belly, and spurred a reckless desire he didn't bother to curb. Not here. Not now.

Not anymore.

Eyes locked, he slid his hand around to the back of her neck and slowly dipped his head toward hers. His thumb nudged her chin up as his mouth descended. To his extreme pleasure, she didn't protest his bold move.

Finally reaching his destination, he ran the tip of his tongue over her lips, flicking teasingly. Her lashes fluttered closed and her lips parted on a soft sigh of surrender that touched him on a dozen different levels. She was so open. So giving. *So trusting.*

The last humbled him, because he knew she'd had little reason to trust lately.

He settled his mouth more fully over hers and deepened the kiss until his tongue tangled with hers. She tasted sweet and warm, like cinnamon and coffee, and he couldn't get enough of her.

Never would.

A moan purred in her throat, and he thought of all the things he'd imagined doing to her earlier, entertained the tempting idea of easing her down onto the mattress and spending the entire day making love to her. That was his libido talking, because at the moment he was hard and aching. Rationally, he knew right now she needed more than physical intimacy. After yesterday, he was more concerned about her emotional stability, and he wouldn't risk more confusion. The next time they made love, he wanted it to be for keeps.

He ended the kiss, slowly dragging his lips from hers.

Wide, luminous eyes stared at him. "What was that for?" She wasn't upset, just curious.

"The hell of it," he replied impulsively. "Because I wanted to. Because you wanted me to. What other reason do I need?"

A smile played at the corner of her mouth. "You're awfully presumptuous."

He gave a deceptively casual shrug. "I've got absolutely nothing to lose."

That truth hung between them, until she finally looked away and plucked absently at the sheet with her fingers. Just as he'd expected, she was going to avoid the personal issues between them. He'd let her be. For now.

Grabbing his own cup of coffee, he took a drink, letting the hot liquid slide down his throat and warm his belly. "So, how are you feeling?" he asked, putting their conversation on a safer track.

She picked at the muffin, and tossed a morsel into her mouth. "Compared to what?"

"To last night."

"Emotionally drained," she said, admitting what he already knew.

He nodded, and wanting to give her something Anthony never had—an apology—he said very quietly, "I'm sorry for losing my temper last night, and for the incident with the gun."

"Apology accepted. And I'm sorry for not listening to your orders." A lopsided smile touched her mouth, diminishing some of the shadows in her gaze. "I think we both were pretty upset after what happened at the beach house, for different reasons."

"Yeah," he agreed, and let it remain at that.

She brushed at the crumbs that had fallen on her T-shirt, and he forcefully pulled his gaze from the way her taut nipples pressed against the soft cotton. He turned, resting his thigh on the bed. The slight shift in position loosened the snug fit of his jeans in a particular region. "Are you up for a little adventure?"

"Are you nuts? I think I've had enough adventure to last me a lifetime, thank you very much."

"Then how do you feel about running away with me for a couple of days?"

Her entire expression lit up, as if he'd given her a huge, gaily wrapped present. "Running away sounds lovely." A frown tugged at her brows, ruining her delight. "Can we do that? I mean, just take off and leave for a couple of days?"

He knew what she was asking, and sought to reassure her. He wanted this weekend to be all pleasure, with little or no thought about the case. "I've already talked to Reynolds about it, and as long as I'm somewhere he can get in touch with me, we're free to go. We'll be back by tomorrow evening." He stopped for a moment to encourage her to eat more muffin, which she did. "I figure you can call Pam and have her handle the boutique while you're gone, and we can stop by the shop on our way out of town so you can pack a few changes of clothes."

She looked impressed, and relieved. "You've thought of everything, haven't you?"

Everything but how I'm going to make you change your mind about us and having a future together. He hoped what he had planned was at least a start in that direction. "I just thought you might like a change of scenery."

"Without a doubt." She smiled around a bite of muffin, then took a drink of coffee. "So, where are we going?"

Her easy acceptance brought him a measure of satisfaction. "It's a surprise, but I guarantee that the food is fabulous, and the atmosphere is total relaxation."

Her eyes rolled back. "God, I'd be a fool to refuse such an invitation."

"I couldn't have said that better myself." She shot him an indignant look for that insult, but he merely grinned. Standing, he set both of their coffee cups on the nightstand and offered her his hand for a boost up. "Come on, lazybones," he teased, feeling more optimistic by the minute. "Let's get you up and dressed so we can blow this joint."

Anticipation touched her features, and she placed her hand in his. "You don't have to ask me twice."

8

PAIGE GUESSED where they were going before they arrived at their destination. He'd taken Interstate 95
north, through Fort Lauderdale, past Palm Beach, to the
small town of Jupiter, where his parents had retired.
The familiar, scenic ride only took a little over an hour,
but as the vehicle ate up each mile away from Miami,
the stress of the past few weeks gradually disappeared.
It was as though Josh was taking her to another world
and she was leaving behind the corruption that had
touched her life.

He'd known just what she'd needed.

She glanced over at him where he sat in the driver's
seat navigating the road, her gaze skimming his strong
profile. "We're going to your parents', aren't we?"

"Yeah." A rakish grin tipped his mouth, and her
heart fluttered in her chest. Josh's lighthearted mood reminded her of simpler times, before her life, her marriage, had started to unravel. "That okay with you?"

She flashed him a reassuring smile. "More than
okay." She looked forward to seeing the older couple
who reminded her so much of her own parents, whom
she missed terribly.

The last time she'd seen Josh's parents had been at
Anthony's funeral, hardly a festive occasion, but they'd
come out of respect, and she'd been grateful for their
support. Anna and Nick Marchiano had attended her

wedding to Anthony, too, and that's where she'd learned that the Marchianos had accepted her husband as one of their own, since Anthony had no family left and Josh had become such a good friend to him. And once she was married to Anthony, Josh's family had welcomed her with the same warmth and kindness they'd instilled in their son. She'd often thought of them as the in-laws she'd never had.

During her first year of marriage to Anthony they'd spent many Sundays and holidays at the Marchianos' for dinner, along with Josh and whoever of his four siblings could attend the gathering. The Marchiano family, she'd discovered, was a large, close-knit, loving Italian family, and she adored every one of them, including Josh's eight little nieces and nephews, who'd automatically given her the honorary title of Aunt Paige.

The second and third year there hadn't been as many visits, and the few she'd managed were without her husband. She'd made excuses for his absence, but she suspected Anna knew something was wrong from the few reproachful comments Paige had overheard Anna making to Josh about Anthony exerting more of an effort to accompany his wife. The other woman's perceptiveness had been startling, though Paige never discussed her marital problems with her.

"How are your parents doing, anyway?" she asked, dragging her thoughts back to a more pleasant topic.

"Okay, I guess." He glanced her way for a moment, and though he wore dark sunglasses, she could feel the warmth of his gaze. "With everything going on the past few months, I've only seen them twice since Christmas." Regret tinged his deep voice.

Knowing that Josh tried to make an effort to have dinner with his parents at least twice a month, Paige understood that he'd been bogged down on the Carranza case. "I bet your mother loves your father being retired, and having so much time to spend with him."

His smile conveyed wry humor. "Mom used to complain that he spent too much time at the station, but she's let a few comments slip about how he's driving her crazy being at home."

Paige laughed. "I'm sure she means it in the most affectionate way possible."

"Probably," he agreed. "But when Dad threatens to go back to the department on a part-time basis, just so he doesn't have to listen to her nag, my mother threatens to divorce him." He shook his head at the incongruity of the situation. "Poor guy can't win."

"It's not easy being married to someone in law enforcement." The defensive statement slipped out before she could think better of it.

He glanced her way. "No, I don't suppose it would be." His response was slow and deliberate, as if he chose his words carefully. "But my mother knew what my dad did for a living before she married him and has lived with it for over forty years."

Feeling an argument rising, Paige declined to comment. Josh certainly knew her feelings on the matter, and she didn't want to rehash issues that neither of them could agree upon.

As she stared out the window and watched the scenery pass, Paige wondered how Anna dealt with the men in her life putting their jobs before family, and decided the woman was a saint to tolerate the stress and worry. She had a husband who'd been with the Fort Lauderdale police department, and her eldest son, Vince, who was married with three children and one on the way, worked for the Jupiter police department.

Though Jupiter was a relatively low-crime community, two years ago he'd been shot in the arm during a convenience-store robbery. The wound hadn't been life-threatening, but Paige clearly remembered how frantic Audrey, Vince's wife, had been over the incident. She also recalled thinking that their three adorable little girls had come too close to losing their daddy.

And then there was Josh, a homicide detective who worked long hours investigating crime scenes and tracing leads, and sacrificed family gatherings for the sake of the job. He didn't put himself in the direct line of fire, not intentionally, but the danger was always there.

The only Marchiano male who hadn't opted for a career in law enforcement was twenty-nine-year-old Joel. He was the smart one, Paige decided—he'd gone into business with a friend and chartered sailboats in St. Lucie. The family affectionately called him the beach bum, and he joked that, with his laid-back life-style, he was going to outlive them all.

Josh's older sister, Tyne, had married a conservative accountant and lived in Orlando with her husband and five children, and Gina, the baby of the family, was still single and working in Tampa as an ad executive. At least Anna didn't have to worry much about her daughters' welfare.

"So, do your mom and dad know we're coming?" she asked curiously.

Josh exited off Interstate 95 and headed east on Indiantown Road to a more remote part of Jupiter. "No. I thought I'd surprise them."

More quietly, she asked, "Do they know about Anthony and this case?"

"Dad does. I told him the last time I came up to visit. I also asked him not to tell Mom." He reached across the console and rested his hand on her thigh. His touch burned through the material of the casual dress she'd donned at the boutique and kicked her pulse up a notch. "Don't worry, he won't put you on the spot with awkward questions. If anything, he'll ask me about the case privately."

"I appreciate that." She didn't mind discussing Anthony's betrayal with Josh, but felt uncomfortable doing so with Nick. "Since your parents aren't expecting us, what are we going to do if they aren't home?"

"I have a key to the house, and we'll be alone." His brows bobbed mischievously. "The possibilities are endless." His voice dropped, filling with sexy male undertones.

Those intimate "possibilities" swirled in her mind, prompting thoughts of the sweet, drugging kiss he'd given her that morning and how reluctant she'd been for it to end. She'd wanted to feel his hands on her breasts, stroking her belly. Wanted him to ease the ache lingering from that strange, erotic dream she'd had before he'd woken her with the delicious smells of breakfast. Even now, she felt unfulfilled, wanting Josh in a way she had no business entertaining. Not when she intended to leave him.

Fifteen minutes later, they arrived at the three-bedroom house Josh's parents had built on a prime piece of land after Nick's retirement from the force five years ago. Ten acres of woods surrounded the charming old-style Victorian home, and a small stable nearby connected to a fenced-in pasture, where two beautiful quarterhorses grazed. The atmosphere was peaceful and serene.

Before either one of them could exit the car, his slender, petite mother was out of the house and heading down the porch stairs. A huge smile wreathed a pretty face framed by short, silky hair the same shade as Josh's, and dark eyes twinkled with pure delight.

"What a lovely surprise!" Reaching Paige as she stepped from the Volvo, the older woman wrapped her in an affectionate hug. "It's so good to see you, dear."

Paige closed her eyes, absorbing the warm embrace before letting the other woman go. She smiled. "It's good to see you, too, Anna."

Anna's gaze narrowed in mock reprimand, and she shook a chastising finger at her. "You haven't visited in months!"

"She's been working too hard," Josh interjected as he rounded the vehicle, saving Paige from fabricating an excuse for her absence. "So I decided to kidnap her and bring her here for some forced R and R."

"And you, Joshua Michael," Anna admonished, turning to her son to give him equal treatment. "You haven't called in weeks, let alone returned the messages I left on your answering machine."

Josh ducked his head sheepishly, making him appear adorably contrite. "I've been busy, Ma."

"Hmmph." Anna's expression softened, but she wasn't completely ready to forgive. "Too busy to call your mother to let her know you're doing okay?"

Josh rolled his eyes and gave Anna a hug that seemed to swallow her up whole within his broad chest, then planted a kiss on her cheek. "Stop already, Ma. You're embarrassing me in front of Paige. I promise it won't happen again."

She gave him a curt, satisfied nod. "Be sure that it doesn't."

"Yes, ma'am," he murmured, shooting Paige a covert, I-can't-believe-she's-doing-this-to-me-in-front-of-you kind of look.

Paige nearly chuckled at Josh's embarrassment, but didn't think he'd appreciate her laughing at his expense. Paige admired the other woman. She certainly knew how to handle her boys and keep them in line—with a firm hand and a loving heart.

"Your father is down in the stables. Go on and get him and don't give him a heart attack by sneaking up on him. He's getting old and isn't as spry as he used to be." She accompanied the outrageous lie with a sly smile and shooed Josh in that direction. "Paige and I are going into the house for a glass of iced tea and some girl talk. I'll call Vince and Joel and see if they can make it for dinner tonight."

"I'd like that." Josh's warm gaze touched on Paige, then returned to his mother. "If you don't mind, Ma, we'd like to stay overnight."

Anna looked properly affronted. "Of course I don't mind! That's what the guest room is for, though you'll be sleeping on the couch."

"That's fine," he conceded with a grin.

Paige followed Anna into her large, spacious kitchen. Anna and Nick lived alone in the custom-built house, but Anna felt that a large cooking and eating area was a necessity, because that's where her family always socialized during get-togethers. Strong family ties, good authentic Italian food and unconditional love were the bonds that held the Marchianos together. Paige loved the other woman's traditional values and how she'd managed to instill in her children the same ideals and morals.

Anna insisted Paige make herself at home, and Paige felt comfortable enough to do so. While she poured each of them a glass of tea, Anna phoned Joel and gave him a similar guilt-inducing spiel about not stopping by often enough when he only lived an hour away. Before she hung up, she'd secured Joel's attendance for dinner. Though Vince was on duty until six that evening, his wife, Audrey, promised to be by soon with the children. Tyne and Gina both lived too far away to make such an impromptu trip.

Anna didn't allow Paige's mind or hands to remain idle, which she silently appreciated. They worked together to prepare dinner while talking companionably about nothing in particular. Anna's idea of "throwing something together" consisted of a huge pot of homemade spaghetti sauce with sausage and her special blend of herbs, her own fresh noodles, a large salad—which had come straight out of her garden—and a loaf of garlic bread. And for dessert, a German chocolate cake made from scratch.

Josh and Nick finally ambled up to the house and into the kitchen, where each of them sampled the various dishes in progress. Anna slapped Nick's hand as he attempted to snag a radish from the salad, and Josh got "the look" from his mother for trying to distract Paige while she frosted the cake so he could sneak a taste of the icing. Apparently, Anna knew how her husband and son operated, and kept an eye on each.

Josh leaned against the counter next to Paige, glanced over his shoulder to make sure his mother was otherwise occupied, and dragged a finger along the rim of the bowl filled with frosting to come away with a big blob of the confection. He popped it into his mouth and winked at her.

Paige couldn't help but grin at his mischievous behavior. "Your mom mentioned German chocolate is your favorite."

"Yep." He swiped another taste. "Are you enjoying yourself?"

"Immensely." She'd been so busy with Anna, she hadn't had time for any unpleasant thoughts. It was a nice change of pace. "Thank you for bringing me here."

"No thanks necessary," he said, his voice low and incredibly gentle. "I'd do anything to keep you smiling, Paige."

Paige's heart swelled at the sweet sentiment, and a lump formed in her throat. If only things were that simple, she thought. If only her life wasn't so complex and she didn't need things Josh couldn't offer her, like stability and security.

He leaned close, so his breath caressed her cheek when he spoke. "Stop thinking so much, sweetheart, because it makes you frown, and I won't allow it this weekend." He followed up that soft demand with a quick, warm kiss on her lips that lingered long after he'd straightened.

Shocked at his brazen display with his parents in the room, Paige's gaze darted to Anna and Nick, who stood by the stove. She felt confident neither of them had witnessed the brief, intimate exchange between her and Josh as Anna was busy feeding her husband a spoonful of the spaghetti sauce and asking for his opinion.

Shaking off the tingling sensation coursing along the surface of her skin, Paige attempted to ignore Josh in hopes that he'd go away. No such luck. He stood there, watching her. Feeling the heat of his gaze on her, she forced herself to concentrate on the task of spreading the frosting evenly on top of the cake. Absently, she ran her tongue across her sticky bottom lip, tasting chocolate and the unique, arousing flavor of Josh. Her stomach tumbled and tightened.

"You've got a little more, right here at the corner," he murmured, slowly gliding his thumb across her mouth. Sure enough, he'd wiped away a smudge of frosting, which he promptly sucked off his thumb, his eyes dark as they held hers.

The breath all but whooshed out of her lungs, and she had the irrepressible urge to throw caution to the wind and give in to the desire that tied her so strongly to Josh—consequences be damned. For weeks she'd resisted him—for years, really—and denying something so intrinsic was becoming more difficult with each passing day. Yet wanting him held so many risks, and the thought of loving him inundated her with so many fears.

Or was it already too late?

Her troubling thoughts dispersed when Josh's younger brother Joel entered the kitchen with a loud, raucous greeting, as was his way. He was tanned a golden brown from the hours he spent outdoors, as good-looking as his two other brothers, and oozed enough sex appeal to charm anyone of the female persuasion.

Paige suspected he'd broken many hearts over the years.

Jovial handshakes and warm hugs went around, and when he came to Paige, his eyes brightened with wicked intent. He swept her dramatically into his embrace, bent her back slightly, and growled playfully into the curve of her neck.

Paige laughed at his outrageous behavior, chalking it all up to Joel's fun-loving personality. Joel's antics seemed to amuse everyone, except Josh. There was a smile on Josh's lips as Joel lifted her back up, his splayed hand supporting the base of her spine, but his eyes blazed with something far more primitive and possessive.

"Watch your hands, little brother." Josh's voice was light and teasing, but not enough to disguise the underlying annoyance vibrating in his tone.

Releasing Paige, Joel lifted one brow in a silent query that went unanswered. Josh's parents shot their older son a speculative look that caused Paige's face to heat, but they, too, refrained from commenting on his odd remark. It wasn't hard to imagine the thoughts racing through everyone's mind.

Shortly thereafter, Audrey, seven months pregnant with her fourth child, arrived with her brood, filling the house with three adorable, energetic little girls ranging in age from four to nine, none of whom had any qualms about clamoring for their uncles' attention, loudly and enthusiastically. Within minutes, the men had spurred the girls into a wild, rambunctious frenzy. Squeals of laughter reverberated in the kitchen, along with the patter of shoes as Joel and Josh instigated a game of tickle monster around the large oak table.

The madness was deafening, crazy and wonderfully distracting.

Anna propped her hands on her slim hips and raised her voice a few decibels to be heard over the noise in her kitchen. "Girls, no running in the house!" Then she turned to her sons. "And since you boys can't behave yourselves either, and seem to be just as bad as the kids, out you go." She hitched a finger toward the back door.

Joel slung an arm over his mother's shoulders, dwarfing her beneath his six-foot-plus height. "Aw, Mom, we're just getting warmed up."

Her mouth pursed and she slanted him a strict look. "Don't 'aw, Mom' me, Joel. You may be able to wrap every other woman around that finger of yours with your sweet-talking charm, but you forget that I've been immune since the day you were born."

He chuckled, but didn't refute that remark.

Josh grinned and headed toward the back door as ordered. "Come on, girls. Let's go feed the horses. I know where Grandpa stashes the sugar cubes."

Three pairs of eyes lit up, and they all scrambled from the kitchen and raced down to the stables as fast as their sneakered feet could carry them. Paige watched from the kitchen window as Joel, Josh and Nick followed at a leisurely pace behind the girls, their male comradery evident in their smiling expressions, deep chuckles and occasional slaps on the back.

"Ah, finally, blessed silence," Audrey said, amusement and relief mingling in her lilting voice. "Now, if I'm real lucky, this little guy will settle down, too." She rubbed her rounded tummy lovingly.

Paige smiled. "So, it's going to be a boy this time?" she asked.

The other woman beamed with happiness and hope. "That's what the sonogram showed, so we've got our fingers crossed. I'm *not* going through this again, not even if we end up with four girls." Blowing out a weary breath, she met Anna's gaze. "Joel isn't the only one good at sweet-talking. He must have taken lessons from Vince."

"It's a Marchiano male attribute, I'm afraid." Anna gave a long-suffering sigh, though the sound was tinged with affection. "Any one of them could cajole candy from a baby."

Paige didn't doubt it—Josh had charm aplenty, as

well as a sensual allure that stirred her in ways no other man ever had. *Irresistible* and *persistent* were apt descriptions for the Marchiano men.

"Why don't the two of you go out on the porch and relax?" Anna suggested in a way that left little room for either of them to protest. "Everything's done here in the kitchen except the cleanup, and I can get it done faster on my own."

Paige and Audrey made their way outside. Settling into the wicker chairs on the porch, they enjoyed the light spring breeze and the sound of children's laughter floating in the air. It was a wonderful sound, Paige thought. So innocent. So trusting. So guileless. It struck a maternal chord in her she found difficult to ignore.

Josh had taken his sports jacket off, along with his shoulder holster and gun—which she assumed he'd put away somewhere safe in the house so the girls wouldn't find the weapon. Gone was the stubborn detective who'd been her bodyguard for the past three weeks, and in his place was a physically fit, gorgeous man who looked carefree and unencumbered by the events of recent weeks.

With a wistful pang near the vicinity of her heart, she watched Josh play ball with his middle niece, Holly, encouraging her when she missed a catch and lavishing praise when she managed to land the ball. In between, he chased after Beth, the youngest, and tossed her into the air until she was breathless with delight. He even managed to tease his oldest niece, Amanda, and tug gently on her pigtails as she fed Desirée, one of the mares in the nearby corral. He clearly adored his nieces, and the feeling appeared mutual. And there was no shortage of attention from Joel, either, who mercilessly tormented the girls with tickling. Both men were totally

at ease with children, which brought to Paige's mind
how impatient Anthony had been with little ones, how
unwilling to interact with them. At the time, she'd written off his remoteness to lack of experience with tod-
dlers, but now understood that children hadn't been a
part of Anthony's plan.

Josh, however, was a natural-born nurturer. Loving.
Kind. Patient. He exhibited those qualities with his
nieces, and he'd displayed them with her, too. Josh was
everything Anthony hadn't been—a tender, giving
lover, a faithful friend, and someone with the potential
to be a caring, loving father.

Her throat closed up, and she blamed the rush of
emotion on the hormonal imbalance that seemed to
have had her in its grip for the past week. She'd been on
an emotional roller coaster and wasn't surprised that
something as simple as witnessing Josh's ease with children would reduce her to a melancholic state.

In the distance she heard a telephone ring. A minute
later, Anna opened the screen door and poked her head
out.

"Audrey, that was Vince on the phone," she said as
she dried her hands on a terry towel. "He wanted to let
you know he'd be a few hours late. He just arrested a
drunk driver and has to get him booked and a report
written."

"Thanks, Anna." Audrey cast the other woman an
easy smile, her hand resting on her distended belly. "If
he doesn't make it for dinner, I'll take some leftovers
home for him."

It amazed Paige that Audrey could sound so matter-
of-fact about Vince's last-minute cancellation. Anthony
had done the same thing, backing out of dates or en-
gagements without warning due to work, or just plain

not showing up for dinner when she'd been expecting him, but she'd never grown used to his erratic schedule.

How did Anna and Audrey make dealing with their husbands' profession look so easy and uncomplicated?

Unable to help herself, she spoke her thoughts out loud. "Don't you ever worry about what Vince does for a living?"

Audrey tilted her head and regarded her speculatively through kind, blue eyes. "That's an odd question coming from someone who was married to a vice cop." Her tone was wry.

She shrugged lightly. "That's probably why I'm more sensitive about it." She'd worried plenty about Anthony's safety, spent too many sleepless nights wondering where he was and if he was okay. And when he didn't come home at the end of his shift, or call, the concern increased to the point of anxiety.

"I used to worry, all the time," Audrey admitted. "But that kind of stress doesn't do me, or the girls, any good." Her gaze touched on the three imps playing a game of freeze tag with Josh and Joel, then traveled back to Paige. Her eyes reflected a deep, abiding love for her family. "I've accepted what Vince does for a living, because I know he loves his job. I would never ask him to choose between me and his career. We've got a strong marriage, and when he's home, he gives me and the girls one hundred percent. That's more than most husbands give their wives and family."

It had been more than Anthony had given her.

"Respect, trust and an open line of communication," Audrey continued wisely. "That's the foundation of any successful marriage. If you have those elements, you can handle any other obstacles that might get thrown into the mix."

Paige desperately wanted to believe the other woman's advice, but her own personal experience had left a bitter taste in her mouth, had hollowed out the depths of her soul.

Her gaze automatically sought out Josh, and he glanced toward the house and waved, a roguish grin canting his mouth. She waved back, unable to stop the wild beating of her heart or the liquid heat that quickened her blood. He had that kind of effect on her senses.

She respected Josh. She trusted him with her life. They communicated on a level she and Anthony hadn't come close to reaching. But after the harsh lessons she'd learned during her marriage to Anthony, Paige realized a greater concern.

She feared she'd be the one who couldn't give Josh the one hundred percent their relationship deserved.

9

UNABLE TO SLEEP, despite how relaxed her body and
mind were, Paige scoured the bookshelf in the guest
bedroom for something to read. She was still basking in
the warmth, teasing and family harmony that had carried through the evening. There was so much love evident in this household, and none of the Marchianos
minded sharing that affection with her. With Anthony,
she'd felt so alone for so long, craving the kind of kin-
ship no phone call home could ease. At least for the
weekend, she felt she belonged to this crazy, loving,
wonderful family. And soon she'd be back in Connecticut with her own parents and siblings.

Skimming past the true-crime paperbacks to the next
row down, Paige selected a short romance novel with a
light premise, propped her pillows against the headboard of her bed and settled in for a few hours' escape.

Minutes later, a quiet knock sounded at the door. Before she could issue an invitation, Josh slipped inside
her room, closing the door soundlessly behind him.
He'd changed from his casual attire of that afternoon
into a pair of soft cotton pajama shorts and nothing else.
His chest was gloriously bare, his body firmly muscled.
Considering he slept beside her in his briefs on a
nightly basis, she would have thought she'd have
grown immune to the sight of his toned body. But it
never failed to elicit a delicious heat and excitement,

and forbidden thoughts that had no business being in her head.

Holding a plate with a slice of German chocolate cake on it, he moved toward the bed. "Hi," he murmured, an irresistible grin curving across his mouth.

The warm, sexy rumble of his voice made her increasingly aware of the skimpy chemise she'd grabbed from the boutique to wear. At the time, she hadn't given much thought to night visitors or bringing along a robe to cover up. The silky material, held up by thin straps, covered her adequately from breast to thigh, yet the snug bodice displayed enough cleavage to draw Josh's eye and make her self-conscious.

"Hi, yourself." Setting the book aside, she tugged her covers a little higher. "Are you sure you should be in here?"

He hesitated at the opposite side of the bed. "Don't you want me here?"

"Of course I want you here," she replied, her response honest. "I always enjoy talking to you. But isn't everyone in bed for the night?"

"Yeah, which means my parents will never know I was here." He sounded like a mischievous little boy getting away with something sneaky. Without asking, he pulled down the covers, fluffed up the pillow and slipped into bed beside her as if he belonged there, all the while balancing that huge piece of cake. Settling in, he shoved a bite into his mouth and chewed. "So, you couldn't sleep either, huh?"

He sat so close, her next breath was filled with the warm, male scent of him. And the fragrance of chocolate. The powerful combination went straight to her head. "No, but I feel totally relaxed."

"That's exactly what I want to hear." He lifted his

fork to her mouth, tempting her with a piece slathered in rich frosting. "Want a bite?" His smile was wolfish and daring.

It wasn't sweets she suddenly craved. "No, thanks. I'm still full from dinner." She watched him devour the slice in record time and shook her head. "Isn't that your third piece tonight?"

"Yeah," he said, unrepentant. The last bite disappeared between his lips and he closed his eyes to savor the taste.

Her gaze dropped to his lips, watching the way his tongue licked away the crumbs and frosting there. Her stomach fluttered and an achy emptiness grew inside her. Struggling to keep her need for this man at bay, she poked him in his firm abdomen and teased, "You'd better be careful, Detective Marchiano, or you're gonna get soft around the middle."

His lashes lifted, and a frown wrinkled his forehead, as if the possibility concerned him. "You think so?"

Her mouth tipped up in a grin. "Keep eating like that and you will."

"No worry there." Setting the plate on the nightstand next to him, he rolled onto his side to face her and propped himself up with his elbow. The movement twisted the covers around his hips, made them slide down to her waist. His dark, smoky eyes didn't miss that fact, or the sight of her nipples beading against silk. "Once we get home I'll be back to my steady regimen of coffee, fruit on the run and prefab microwave dinners, when I remember to eat." He rubbed his flat belly. "That bland diet always keeps me fit and trim."

"Microwave dinners?" Infusing her tone with feigned pity, she reached out and with her palm, caressed the light stubble lining his jaw. "Aww, poor baby."

He caught her hand before she could withdraw it, and just like that, the spark between them flared to life. She saw the magical awareness in his gaze, felt it in the subtle tightening of her body. His eyes seemed to pull her into their golden depths, seducing her, leaving her breathless with anticipation.

Bringing her fingers to his lips, he touched the tips with his tongue, let his warm breath caress the dampness. A delicious shiver raced up her arm, pooled heavily in private places.

That lazy smile of his slowly eased up the corner of his mouth. "If you genuinely felt sorry for me, you'd marry me and make sure I got three healthy meals a day." His voice held an odd tightness, despite its casual, humorous tone.

A growing pressure banded her chest, painful in its intensity. She wanted to believe he was joking, but knew beneath all that charm and seduction his words were as serious as an out-and-out proposal. She let him down as gently as possible. "You wouldn't be home most of the time to eat dinner, let alone breakfast and lunch."

He absently stroked the inside of her wrist with his thumb, generating tiny circles of heat. "If I had you to come home to, you could bet I'd make every effort to enjoy every meal and then some."

Sadness and regret flickered through her. "That kind of devotion ends once the honeymoon is over."

Promises of forever shimmered in his gaze. "It doesn't have to."

"In my experience, it does," she argued.

Somewhere along the way, their conversation had

taken a personal spin, their words filled with meaning. Josh wanted her in his life, intimately and permanently; she couldn't bring herself to commit her heart and soul, and a man like Josh would accept no less.

He didn't push the issue, though she caught a fleeting glimpse of frustration in his expression. He released her hand, severing the tie between them, and Paige felt as though she were adrift, with no anchor in sight. She fought an overwhelming urge to cry for everything she'd lost in that single moment and blamed it on those unruly hormones flowing through her body.

He pulled in a deep breath and eased it out just as slowly, seemingly searching for his own stable ground. "Joel seemed awfully attentive with you today," he commented.

That made her smile, because he sounded and looked so sullen—like a child who'd had his favorite toy taken away. "Joel is always an outrageous flirt. You're just being more sensitive than normal."

"Am I?" His brows lowered into the same scowl he'd shot at his brother a few times that evening.

"Yeah, you are." She ruffled his thick, silky hair, loving the feel of the warm strands sliding through her fingers. "I never thought you were the jealous type."

"I've never had a reason to be. Until now." His voice was slightly rough, a ragged kind of velvet that was as dark and soft as the night. "I'm finding that I don't like the thought of another man touching you."

His gaze trapped her, holding her hostage as they teetered on the sharp edge of a very sensitive issue. When she found her voice again, she replied, "That's awfully possessive."

He shrugged a shoulder, the look in his eyes unapologetic. "Yeah, I suppose it is. But that's the way I feel about you, all the more so because I stand the chance of losing you."

Her heart stopped, then resumed at a breakneck pace. She saw the determination glowing in his gaze, and undiluted panic raced through her blood, filling every pore with a throbbing, aching kind of fear.

"I love you, Paige," he said, low and fierce.

Oh, Lord, she'd known that was coming, thought she'd prepared herself to hear those three little words from Josh and not let her need and yearning interfere with her self-control. She shook her head in a frantic attempt to stop the rush of emotion bubbling to the surface. "Josh, no," she forced out, her voice choked.

"More than friends," he went on with a tender ruthlessness, ignoring her plea. "More than acquaintances." In a blur of movement she couldn't have anticipated, he grasped her hips and dragged her closer, until his body pressed against her side and his face loomed above hers. Her hands automatically caught his arms, holding on as uncertainty played havoc with her mind.

Male heat radiated from him, raw and untamed. He locked his gaze with hers, the intensity in the depths of those amber orbs shaking her resolve. "*I love you.*"

A shudder ripped through her, stripping away the protective layers she'd secured around her heart. She had no defenses when it came to Josh. Her need and desire for him was too strong to deny, and she suspected he knew it, too.

Tears stung her eyes. The reciprocating words jammed in her throat, wouldn't pry loose. Knowing no other way to express her feelings, she slid her fingers into his thick hair, brought his mouth to hers and kissed him with all the love that crowded her heart to overflowing—for him.

He groaned at the first touch of her lips on his, the sound encouraging her. His strong body shuddered when she boldly stroked her tongue against his. From there he took over, responding to the fevered heat burning between them. He kissed her just as deeply, just as demandingly. Neither could get enough of the other, their hunger and need an insatiable thing.

Hard and urgent eventually gave way to soft and exploring. Time slipped away as they indulged in every kind of kiss imaginable. Languid, drugging kisses. Tender, cherishing kisses. Deep, wet, slippery kisses that made her melt. Sexy, erotic kisses that elicited a greater need and urged her to move shamelessly against him.

With his mouth still fused to hers, he shifted, slipping a hard thigh between hers. She welcomed the pressure, gasped when he rubbed sensuously against that tender nub of flesh that throbbed so insistently at the apex of her thighs.

Her body quickened and her hips undulated. She made a desperate sound, tightened her thighs around his and arched, but she couldn't get close enough. Oh, God, had she ever needed anything so badly? Her breath came in heavy pants, and she tore her mouth from Josh's. His dark eyes reflected the same passion thrumming through her veins.

"Josh..." Confusion and wanting thickened her voice.

"Shh..." Tangling his fingers into her hair, he lowered his head to feather more kisses over her lips, her jaw, her throat, drawing a moan of pleasure from her. "We're just kissing and touching," he murmured, nuzzling her neck, then lapping his tongue over the pulse fluttering at the base. "Feels good, doesn't it?"

Better than good, she thought. Closing her eyes, she cradled his face in her hands and brought his lips back to hers, answering his question with a lazy, open-mouthed, tongue-tangling kiss. The hand on her hip roamed, sliding upward over silk. He pushed aside the thin strap of her chemise, eased it down her shoulder and cupped the heavy weight of her breast in his palm.

She sucked in a sharp breath when his thumb flicked over her taut nipple. Her breasts felt swollen, heavy, too sensitive. He lightened his touch, brushed his knuckles over the velvety crest to soothe the ache, but even that simple caress electrified her nerve endings. She couldn't stop the whimper that escaped her throat.

He lifted his head and looked at her, concern knitting his brows. "Are you okay?"

She bit her lower lip and nodded, unwilling to voice her suspicions about *why* her breasts ached. Remembering what had happened the last time they'd been in such a compromising position on a bed, she lifted the strap of her chemise back where it belonged and said, "I don't think this is such a good idea."

He gave her a lopsided smile. "I think it's a great idea, but I understand." Reluctantly, he moved back to his side of the bed. "I guess we ought to call it a night."

She nodded her agreement, already missing the warmth of his body next to hers. Regretting, too, that the evening had to end this way.

Picking up his plate, he headed for the door. Hand on the knob, he hesitated and glanced back at her. His gaze was fierce as it held hers. And incredibly warm. "I meant what I said earlier, Paige. I love you." Then he was gone.

Emotion welled inside her and she tried not to cry at the hopelessness of their situation, but lost the battle. A lone tear trickled down her cheek and she whispered to the empty, lonely room what she couldn't bring herself to say to Josh. "I love you, too. More than friends. More than acquaintances."

She always would.

"So, YOU WANT to tell me what's going on between you and Paige?" Nick asked the question as they each saddled up a horse for the early-afternoon ride Josh planned to take Paige on before they headed back to Miami. "Besides you guarding her until the case is over?"

Josh slanted his father a wry look, wondering where that insightful question had come from. Since Paige was up at the house helping his mother clean up after lunch, he felt relatively safe in discussing the subject. "Are my feelings that obvious?"

Nick shrugged his broad shoulders as he fitted a saddle onto Desirée's back. "I know you've always cared for her, but your mother and I were talking last night and we both sense something between the two of you has changed. Has it?"

"My feelings for Paige have grown over the years," he admitted, unable to deny the truth to his father. "But I never would have acted upon them with her being married to Anthony. Now that he's gone, I think we've both realized there's more to our relationship than just being friends." Coaxing Paige into admitting those emotions, though, was another thing. The kiss she'd instigated last night spoke volumes, but it wasn't enough, not when he wanted forever with her.

"What are you going to do about it?" Nick asked after a quiet moment had passed.

"I honestly don't know." Josh tightened the girth on

Lacey's saddle, then gave her an affectionate rub along her sleek neck. "Anthony didn't leave Paige with the best impression of being a cop's wife, and I'm finding it difficult to compete with those bad memories."

Understanding glimmered in Nick's gaze. "Not everyone is cut out to be a cop's wife. You know that as well as I do."

"Mom did it," Josh stated, not wanting to think about the high divorce rate within their profession.

"Your mother could have been a sergeant herself."

Josh chuckled. Despite his father's grumblings, there was no doubt in Josh's mind that Nick's comment was spoken with respect and adoration for the woman who'd put her husband and family above all else. And Nick had been just as loyal and dedicated. Their marriage had been a mutual compromise, a case of give-and-take.

Not so in Paige's case. She'd given and Anthony had taken, leaving Paige empty and stung by several different forms of betrayal. Was it no wonder she was so distrusting of her feelings?

"Your mother and Paige come from two different backgrounds," Nick went on as they led the two mares from the stable and out into the warm sunshine. "Anna grew up the oldest in a household. She was only ten when her mother died, and raising her younger brothers and sisters made her older and wiser than her years. By the time I met her, she'd already developed that take-charge kind of personality. She has an inner strength few women possess."

Josh firmly believed Paige had that emotional fortitude within her as well. It might have withered from Anthony's manipulative abuse and neglect, but hadn't she demonstrated that courage when she'd made the decision to leave Anthony and demanded a divorce that last day they'd been together? She hated the situation Anthony had unwittingly dragged her into, but she'd dealt with Carranza and Bridget with an intrepidness that had made him proud.

Oh, yeah, she had more courage than she realized, or gave herself credit for. But it was up to Paige to see that strength within herself. Embrace it. Believe in it. It wasn't something he could force upon her.

Nick looped Desirée's reins around the second rung of the fence bordering the corral as they waited for Paige to arrive. "Your mother and I have gone through our share of problems," Nick went on, gazing up at the house. "Some of them stemmed from my job as a cop, but when you love someone as much as I love your mother, you put your priorities in order and make it work."

Josh had watched Paige struggle to keep her marriage to Anthony together, but without two people striving toward a common goal, it had been impossible. And as the old saying went, she was once burned, twice shy.

Lacey snorted softly and nudged Josh in the shoulder for some attention. Josh scratched her behind the ear. A few minutes later, Paige came out of the house and headed toward the stable, a relaxed smile on her face. Black stirrup pants molded to her slender legs, and an over-sized T-shirt reached to mid-thigh, hiding the more generous curves of her body. She'd pulled her auburn hair into a ponytail and wore little makeup. He couldn't remember the last time she'd looked so refreshed and beautiful, and knew the easy, unhurried atmosphere was the reason.

Having grown up with horses, Paige slid gracefully into Desirée's saddle. Josh followed suit with Lacey.

"Have a good time, you two," his father said with a wave, then headed back toward the house.

Josh guided the horses toward a dirt path that led to the edge of the wooded area surrounding his parents' house. The sun shone bright and warm, the air fresh and sweet as it carried on the slight breeze.

Paige drew a deep breath and let it out on a blissful sigh. Her body rocked in the saddle, flowing with the horse's movements. "Can we stay here forever?"

Josh was tempted to say yes, just to keep that dazzling smile on her lips. "We can always come back. Anytime."

She glanced at him, regret clouding her gaze, telling him she still planned on leaving him after her part in the case was over. "Your parents' place reminds me of home. Laid-back. Casual. None of the hustle of the city. I can't tell you how much I miss that." Reaching down, she stroked Desirée's withers. "I always thought I'd marry someone from Connecticut, maybe settle down on a farm, have half a dozen kids..." Her voice trailed off wistfully.

"And instead you moved to Miami and married Anthony."

"Didn't think twice about it, either," she said, not without a note of self-recrimination. "I loved him, Josh, and I honestly believed he loved me, too. I wouldn't have married him otherwise." She gave a humorless laugh. "Unfortunately, I was wrong about Anthony's intentions."

Josh's jaw tightened. "Anthony didn't know how to appreciate what he had."

She shrugged, resignation in her expression. "What I

wanted was so simple, really. A faithful husband, a warm home filled with love and laughter, a family of my own. The kind of things most women want, I suppose."

"I want to give you those things, Paige."

Her fingers tightened on the reins. "And I want those things with you, too, Josh, but I hate what you do for a living, the danger, the uncertainties—"

"Then I'll find another job." The words spilled out automatically, desperately, without thought. His heart thudded as he waited for her answer, because he wasn't sure if he could give up something that was so much a part of him.

She understood. "No, you won't, because I'd never ask you to do that for me. You honestly love what you do, and I respect that, but I can't live with it again. The long hours, the sleepless nights...the fear of loving someone I might lose."

Frustration twisted inside him. "Life, or marriage, doesn't come with guarantees. You won't find them with me or anyone else."

Sadness dimmed her green eyes. "Oh, I know that, but I can lessen the risk."

Josh's mood veered sharply to anger. He damned Anthony for tainting her perception of being a cop's wife. Mostly, he damned himself for not being more assertive three years ago and laying his own claim to Paige.

Now it was too late.

"Josh...I started my period this morning," she said quietly.

The finality of her statement sent a shaft of disappointment straight through his heart. In the deepest recesses of his soul, he realized he'd been hoping that she'd be pregnant with their baby, which would have kept her bound to him in ways his declaration of love couldn't. Selfish, yes, but the thought of losing her tied him up in knots.

He tried to separate his anticipation from more immediate concerns. "Do we need to make a quick trip to the store?"

A small smile played around the corners of her mouth, but didn't diminish the shadows in her eyes. "I had a feeling I was going to start soon and came prepared. I think getting away from everything finally alleviated the stress my mind and body have been under."

"Yeah, you're probably right." His voice was rough, and he swallowed to ease the dryness.

"It's for the best, Josh."

He forced himself to nod. "You certainly don't need the worry of being pregnant right now."

"No, I don't," she agreed, staring toward the open field of tall grass and wildflowers stretching ahead. "Another week, two at the most, and I'll be back in Connecticut."

Without him. Josh's chest tightened and his mind sifted through the dozen different ways he could coerce Paige into remaining in Florida with him and marrying him. Desperate thoughts. Self-indulgent thoughts.

He didn't voice any of them. If he pressured her to stay, she'd be miserable, possibly grow to resent him, and he'd be no better than Anthony, who'd had no qualms about manipulating her emotions.

The decision to remain had to be made of her own free will.

He loved her and there was only one thing he could do to prove how much he cared.

He'd let her go.

10

PAIGE HUNG UP the phone in her office, her hand amazingly steady considering her insides were trembling with an abundance of nerves. Remaining behind her desk, she glanced over at Josh and the high-tech recording equipment he'd set up to monitor every incoming and outgoing call on her business line since Monday. Wednesday had finally produced the results they'd been anticipating.

They'd been expecting the call from Carranza. Josh had briefed her on possible situations and answers, so she'd been prepared to handle whatever direction Victor chose to take the conversation. She'd been calm and poised during their verbal exchange, had even managed to interject light laughter at the appropriate times. The man had been charming and straightforward in his approach, stating a further interest in the Wild Rose, and the diamond-and-emerald necklace she had in her possession. He wanted to discuss both at the dinner party he'd invited her and her "companion" to.

His interest in her boutique was merely a smoke screen, she knew, and the idle comment he'd made about having his jeweler duplicate the emerald necklace if she wasn't willing to part with hers was a nice, reassuring touch, she thought.

Josh pushed a button to stop the recording tape and

slipped off the headset he wore. His gaze met hers, warm and encouraging. "You did great, Paige."

"Well, it sounds like we have ourselves a date for Saturday evening. A black-tie affair, no less. I guess this means I'll be getting a new dress for the occasion." A forced smile curved her lips, but did nothing to veil the edge of sarcasm in her voice. "And I thought it was quite generous of Carranza to offer us weekend access to his guest cottage, didn't you?"

Josh stood and stretched, his gaze turning cautious. "If everything goes as planned, we won't be there beyond Saturday evening."

She gathered the inventory sheets she'd been working on before Carranza had called and stuffed them into a file folder. Between her contact with Victor, and the earlier conversation she'd had with her Realtor with regard to a solid offer on the beach house—a discussion Josh had heard word for word, including the fact that she'd accepted the bid without hesitation—Paige's concentration was shot. "*If* leaves a large margin for error, Marchiano. What if the entire weekend is a complete bust and nothing happens? Then what?"

"Then, come Monday morning, we'll be sending you back home to Connecticut." His gaze searched her face, as if committing every feature to memory. "No matter what happens this weekend, by Monday evening you'll be back home with your family, where you want to be."

The folder in her hand slipped to the desk, and a huge lump formed in her throat. "What?" she breathed, unable to believe what she'd just heard.

"I'm not willing to risk your life any more than we already have, and I've told Reynolds as much." He opened a black case and began putting the recording equipment away. "I don't even want to put you through this weekend, but we all know if we backed out now it would look suspicious and we'd lose whatever ground we've gained. And we may never get another chance to get as close to Carranza as this weekend will allow." He glanced up at her, a powerful combination of gentleness and determination darkening his eyes. "You understand that, don't you?"

"Yes." She understood that he regretted the situation she'd been forced into because of Anthony. And, as a result, he'd been thrust into the danger, too. Together, they'd do whatever was necessary to put an end to Carranza's exploits. They had no choice.

"And with luck, Carranza will attempt to seize the necklace while we're there. If not, I've already talked to Reynolds about your leaving after this weekend, and he's making all the necessary arrangements to make sure you get home safely and have the protection you need until Carranza is arrested."

More than words could express, she appreciated the efforts he'd made to grant her wish to return home. They hadn't spoken of their relationship since returning from his parents', but his eyes reflected his emotions, and so did his actions.

He truly loved her, more than Anthony ever had. He was letting her go, giving her what she said she wanted.... So why did she feel she was making the biggest mistake of her life?

Shaking off the question that had begun to haunt her, she left her desk and approached Josh, rerouting her thoughts back to the case. "If Carranza isn't apprehended this weekend, what will happen with him and the necklace?"

"We have a fence who is currently working with the police, and we'll have to filter the necklace through him and have Carranza believe that you've sold it." Closing the lid on the black case, he secured the locks, then faced her. "It'll be more difficult to apprehend Carranza, and will take longer than we'd anticipated, but I'm not willing to risk your safety beyond this weekend." His jaw clenched fiercely.

They stood so close, she ached to reach out and touch him, but didn't dare for fear of doing something incredibly stupid…like kissing him as she'd been longing to since their return trip from his parents'.

"I want him caught, Josh." This horrible nightmare wouldn't end for her just because she was safe in Connecticut, not when Josh's life was still at stake. She'd worry endlessly about him as long as Carranza remained a free man. "I'd like to see him, and Bridget, behind bars this weekend."

"That's what we're hoping for, too." The first smile she'd seen in days kicked up the corner of his mouth, softening his expression. "We'll be on Carranza's turf, and our guess is that's where he'll most likely make his move to obtain the necklace, though we can't predict how or when he'll approach you, which is the difficult part."

She drew a deep breath, resigned to what she had to do, despite her aversion to the situation. Both of their lives depended on her cooperation, and her ability to anticipate the grimmest of circumstances. "Then prepare me for the worst."

Bracing his hands on his hips, he stared at her for a long moment, a spark of admiration entering his gaze. "All right. I want you to make arrangements to have Pam run the store so your days will be freed up."

"She's agreed to manage the boutique until it sells," she said, having already discussed her plans to leave

Miami with Pam. It had been a tearful, emotion-filled conversation, but ultimately Pam had understood her decision, and had already begun to take charge of the day-to-day business dealings. "I'm hoping the new owner, whoever it is, will keep her on."

Josh nodded. "Over the next three days, we'll practice self-defense maneuvers, and we'll spend a few hours each day at the shooting range so you'll feel comfortable with Liz's derringer."

The apprehension Paige thought she'd experience never materialized. It was as though her acceptance had bolstered her courage, made her stronger internally, and pushed aside all uncertainties. She could do this, she realized, as long as she kept her focus. "Okay."

"I'm taking the tape that recorded your call with Carranza to Reynolds, and he can use it to brief our officers who'll be working undercover this weekend. We've already discovered who is catering the party and assigned men to stand in as part of the crew. Same with the valet service. We've been able to post at least two dozen officers at Carranza's estate for Saturday night."

Paige's mind spun with all the information he offered, and she struggled to absorb it all.

He went on. "You'll also be sitting in on any briefings so you'll know exactly what our strategy will be, how our men will be set up, and what will happen when Carranza makes his move for the necklace." His eyes narrowed shrewdly. "The next three days will be intense. Are you up for that?"

"Yes," she said, meaning it.

A satisfied light came into his gaze. "Then let's get started."

SATURDAY AFTERNOON, Paige and Josh headed across the Rickenbacker Causeway to Carranza's private estate in Key Biscayne. Despite the unpredictability of what lay ahead, Paige felt surprisingly calm, and knew Josh was the reason for her stable frame of mind. For the past three days, he'd committed himself to preparing her both mentally and physically for any confrontation she might possibly face, at times pushing her to the edge of exhaustion and frustration. Still, she'd endured his vigorous demands, knowing the skills he taught her would keep them alive. She'd learned to decipher subtle cues from Josh, knew how to fire a derringer blindfolded, and mastered half a dozen ways to incapacitate a person.

She would wear the Ivanov necklace and knew exactly how to handle any encounter with Carranza or his supposed appraiser. The wireless microphone that had been sewn into the bodice of the gown she'd wear tonight—along with the one Josh would use—was a bit of security Reynolds had insisted upon, just in case she and Josh were separated. The undercover officers would be outfitted with receivers, enabling them to hear their conversations throughout the evening.

Between those lessons and the briefings with Reynolds and the officers assigned to the case, Josh had helped her pack up personal items from the beach house. She'd hired professional movers to secure the rest of her possessions and furniture, and ship them on to Connecticut. By Monday, the house would be empty and she would be gone.

For the past week, she and Josh had been living in a two-bedroom furnished apartment that rented by the week. By the time they arrived home in the evenings after a full day of training and review of strategies, she was so exhausted she fell into bed and slept soundly until dawn. Their hectic schedule left little time for idle conversation, and as a result they didn't talk about her move back to Connecticut. Not that there was anything left to say. She was leaving and Josh was letting her go, giving her what she said she ultimately wanted.

With every day that passed, she ached at the thought of losing Josh, a man who'd given her friendship, had been her lover in the darkest hours of need, and still remained steadfast and true. Yet she feared what her heart was telling her—feared trusting her feelings, believing she and Josh could have a solid, secure future together. Past experience had taught her otherwise.

At the entrance to Carranza's estate, Josh announced their arrival. After a brief moment, the elaborate wrought-iron gates slowly opened, allowing them access, and he guided the Volvo up the winding, private road. The scenery, left Paige breathless in awe. The estate, a paradisical hideaway, was surrounded by rolling green lawn and lush, vibrant landscaping. Beyond, she could see the tropical blue water of the Atlantic Ocean.

"Are you ready for this?" Josh asked, slowing the vehicle as the driveway circled around an elaborate marble fountain, then ended in front of a graceful, elegant mansion that seemed to go on forever.

Watching as a uniformed valet approached their idling car, Paige drew a deep breath and flashed Josh a smile. "As ready as I'll ever be."

"Good." His voice was a low, husky murmur in the close confines of the car, his gaze just as sexy and intimate. He reached out and brushed his fingers along her cheek, tucked a wisp of hair behind her ear—all part of the pretense of being lovers, she assumed, yet that didn't stop her pulse from leaping or her skin from heating.

He cast a surreptitious glance at the man striding toward her side of the car. "The guest cottage will most likely be bugged, so once we leave this car, there will be no more talk of the case, okay?"

She licked her suddenly dry lips and nodded. "All right."

His fingers slipped to the base of her neck and an involuntary shiver rippled through her. He looked as if he wanted to kiss her, looked as if he wanted to say more, but there was no time.

The valet opened the passenger door, interrupting the moment. "Good afternoon, ma'am," he said pleasantly.

Josh let go of her, slowly sliding his hand away, and she turned her attention to the man waiting to help her from the vehicle. Placing her fingers in his white-gloved ones, she slipped from her seat and stood, wondering if this clean-cut young man was on their side or Carranza's.

"Thank you," she murmured, retrieving her hand from his as quickly as possible. At the moment, she didn't trust anyone but Josh. So as not to appear anxious, she smoothed a hand down the chocolate-colored, knee-length silk dress she'd worn. The gown was one she'd taken from the boutique's inventory, simple in design, yet sexy in a body-forming way. Perfect for a weekend tryst, Pam had told her, as she'd selected a pair of heeled sandals and some matching lingerie that Paige had been skeptical about wearing.

Standing a few feet away, she waited while the young man unloaded their one suitcase and garment bag and placed them on the imported tile veranda in front of the main door. He rang the doorbell, caught the keys Josh tossed his way, hopped into the Volvo and drove it around a bend in the drive Paige hadn't noticed until then. She supposed with all the parties Carranza threw, he had a separate lot to park his guests' cars.

By the time she and Josh made their way up the steps to the veranda, the front door had opened and a staid-looking butler greeted them. Another man dressed in black slacks, a crisp white shirt and black bow tie whisked their luggage away. Paige experienced a moment of panic, until she remembered that Josh had placed the velvet-lined bag holding the Ivanov necklace in her purse for just such a reason. Her hand tightened on the strap.

The older, gray-haired butler escorted them through a marbled foyer and into a large room decorated in rich furnishings. A small gathering of people milled about, talking and laughing, indulging in the wine and the light buffet spread out on a nearby mahogany sideboard. By the time Paige found Carranza and Bridget across the room, the other man had spotted her. Paige looped her arm through Josh's, as much for silent support as to give the impression they were lovers.

Victor excused himself from the couple he was talking to and approached her and Josh. Bridget remained behind, casually sipping her glass of wine, but her cold, assessing gaze raked over Paige, then went on to scrutinize Josh. Josh merely smiled at the viperous woman, then turned his attention to Victor. He shook his hand as Paige made the introductions, using the false last name of Bennett that Josh had established as part of his cover.

Carranza smiled amicably, the expression in his dark eyes just as gracious, as he welcomed them to his home. Paige marveled at this man's ability to appear so friendly and hospitable when she knew a ruthless criminal lurked beneath that pleasant facade. Victor spent the next half hour acquainting her and Josh with the other couples in the room, all of whom Paige found to be pretentious and snooty, then finally drew them toward the sideboard of appetizers and gestured for them to help themselves.

Paige was too nervous to eat and politely declined, but Josh had no qualms about sampling the delicacies.

Victor plucked a large shrimp from a tray and dipped it into the accompanying cocktail sauce. "You did bring the necklace, I hope?" Victor asked, his tone deceptively casual.

"Yes." She smiled, miffed at Josh's ability to eat when her stomach was in knots. He pretended disinterest in her conversation with Carranza, but she knew he was listening and alert. "I'll be wearing it tonight."

"Wonderful. My appraiser is looking forward to seeing it." Victor glanced at the huge gilded grandfather clock that dominated a corner of the room, then back at them. "I'm expecting about a hundred guests for dinner this evening, and they'll be arriving right up to six o'clock, when cocktails and appetizers will be served. You have three hours to play or relax, the choice is yours. You're welcome to use the pool, or explore the grounds, or stay here and mingle."

Three hours of polite talk wasn't an option for Paige. "If you don't mind, I think I'd like to take a nap. I've had a headache that I can't seem to shake." She pressed her fingers to her temples for emphasis and offered a smile. "A few aspirins and a nap ought to take care of it."

Josh strummed his fingers lightly down her spine and leaned close. "I'll take care of that headache for you, sweetheart," he murmured, his warm breath caressing the curve of her neck.

Carranza, having heard Josh's remark, smirked. "You'll find the guest cottage fully stocked, so please enjoy the amenities."

Josh's large, masculine hand skimmed boldly over her bottom in sexual implication. "Oh, I'm certain we will."

Paige struggled to catch her breath. Josh might be acting, but his lusty performance sparked a very real desire within her.

Carranza gave the butler a discreet nod. "Have Henry take Mrs. Montgomery and her guest to the west guest cottage."

"Yes, sir," the butler replied formally, and after motioning to the same man who'd taken their baggage earlier, he relayed the directions Victor had just given him.

Ten minutes later, she and Josh were alone inside an elegantly furnished cottage. Their accommodations consisted of a stocked kitchen and dining area, a luxurious living room with a big-screen TV, a bedroom twice the size of her own and a decadent bathroom complete with a Jacuzzi bath and a large, tiled shower stall. The cottage was situated at least two hundred yards away from the main house and right on its own private beach.

Josh switched on the elaborate stereo system in the living room to help drown out any noise they made or conversations they had. Soft rock music filtered through the cottage, familiar and soothing. Paige wandered into the bedroom, set her purse on the dresser, then opened the sliding glass door to let fresh air circulate through the room. She gazed out at the ocean while Josh inspected closets, drawers and other places for possible hidden listening devices. He found none, but they both knew that meant nothing.

"When our host mentioned amenities, he wasn't kidding," Josh said as he returned to the bedroom, amusement lightening his tone. "There's everything from adult videos, to a fully stocked bar, to a box of condoms in the nightstand."

She glanced over her shoulder and lifted a brow. "The hospitality here is overwhelming."

He grinned, his eyes dancing with humor as he approached. His hands came to rest on her shoulders, and he massaged the tense muscles there with skillful ease. Her head fell forward and she groaned, feeling the stress drain from her body with every deep stroke of his thumbs along her neck.

"Now, about that headache…"

She shivered at the husky timbre of his voice and turned around, intending to tell him it had been an excuse to escape three hours of awkward pleasantries, but the knowing look in his golden-brown eyes cut her off. He touched his fingertips to her mouth, a gentle caress, and a huge ache yawned inside her.

She knew the sexual advances he'd made in Carranza's presence were meant to establish the illusion of being intimate. Even now, Josh's words and actions were chosen for the benefit of any listening ears. Yet as their eyes met, a hungry awareness swirled between them. She experienced a desperate urge to make love with Josh, to give him everything welling inside her, and take just as much.

She had no idea what tonight would hold, or what tomorrow would bring. More than anything, she wanted this one last time with him to take with her and remember when she was alone and missing him. She wanted to feel loved and cherished. No promises. No regrets.

"Paige..." His voice vibrated with uncertainties, though his gaze was fever-bright with desire.

"I want this. I need this," she whispered, then gathered her courage to admit her strongest weakness, her greatest fear. *"I need you."*

Not giving him a chance to reject her, she cupped his jaw between her cool palms, brought his mouth to hers and kissed him, pouring every emotion she felt for him into that fusing of lips, that tangling of tongues. He didn't deny her, but then she knew he would never refuse anything she asked, not if her request was within his power to grant.

His selflessness made her love him all the more.

Her hands skimmed down his neck and slipped into the collar of his sports jacket, tugging it over his shoulders, down his arms, and letting it fall to the floor. He wasn't wearing his shoulder holster, but she knew he wasn't without a weapon. She continued to kiss him, aggressively, endlessly, searing her senses and inflaming them both. The thought of the impending danger they faced made her need for him more vital. Her fingers fluttered to the buttons on his shirt, but he caught her hands before she could part the material.

He tore his mouth from hers, his breathing harsh. "Give me a minute," he murmured, his voice rough with arousal.

Those sixty seconds felt like an eternity to Paige. She watched him toe off his loafers, then bend down, lift his right pant leg and hastily remove the holster he'd secured there. He withdrew a snub-nosed revolver, set it on the nightstand next to the bed, and returned to her, his eyes glowing with golden heat and promise. Plowing all ten fingers into her hair, he closed his mouth over hers, picking up where they'd left off with a long, greedy kiss she returned with equal fervor.

Within seconds, they were wild and on fire for each other. Paige knew this wouldn't be a gentle loving; what she longed for was fierce and primitive, and Josh was well on his way to giving her the untamed joining her heart and body clamored for.

She nearly tore off his shirt in her haste to touch bare skin. He shrugged out of the garment, and she rubbed her palms over his chest, dizzied by the feel of heat and muscle. She skimmed lower, over his flat belly to the waistband of his pants, struggling to unbuckle his belt. An encouraging moan purred in her throat when he reached behind her, unzipped her dress, and trailed his fingers down the ever-widening path to the base of her spine. She lowered her arms, and the silky fabric slid down her body and pooled around her feet, leaving her scantily clad in wispy cocoa-colored panties and a matching sheer lace bra. His pants and briefs quickly followed.

He reached to pull her close, to rid her of her lingerie, but she had other ideas. She broke their kiss and looked her fill of him, savoring every inch of his naked body. And he let her, though she knew by the tense set of his jaw it took incredible restraint. He was a gorgeous man, his body honed and tightly muscled. She stroked the breadth of his shoulders, touched her fingertips to his chest, lightly circled his navel…and explored lower, her gaze inexorably drawn to the thick arousal jutting from the nest of dark hair between his thighs.

Before she reached her destination, however, he grasped her wrist and jerked her hand away. "Paige, I can't take much more," he said gruffly.

She licked her dry lips, moistening them with her tongue. Her heart pounded in her chest as she thought of all the things she wanted to do to him. With him. Erotic things to remember for a lifetime. "Let me touch you," she whispered. "Please."

His eyes darkened, and she knew he wouldn't refuse her provocative request. But she never could have anticipated his next move. Holding her gaze with his, he lifted her hand to his lips and sucked each one of her fingers into his mouth, thoroughly wetting them, then slid his soft tongue over her palm. Her stomach clenched and she grew damp, liquid, ready.

Lowering her lubricated hand, he wrapped her fingers around his straining shaft. She stroked his rigid length with her slick palm and he grasped her face between his large hands and kissed her, slipping his tongue deep within her mouth, enticing her with his own brand of seduction. And with each silken glide of her fingers he grew impossibly harder, thicker....

He groaned helplessly and lifted his mouth from hers. "Too fast," he muttered, stopping the motions of her hand.

She was breathing hard, her pulse racing. Yes, she did feel a little out of control, but she reveled in the uninhibited sensation. Her heart hammered, with excitement, anticipation and an urgency he instinctively understood.

With a dark oath, his mouth descended once again, crushing hers in a lush, rapacious kiss as he guided her back until her spine was flattened against the cool wall and his hot body pressed intimately into hers. He buried his face into the curve of her neck and she arched into him, gasping when his erection slid against the silk covering her mound. She moaned and tilted her hips, needing him inside her, half out of her mind for him to ease the building ache there.

"Josh, now," she begged, moving shamelessly against him.

"Not yet," he breathed hotly against her skin. Grasping the straps of her bra, he pulled them down her arms, just until her breasts sprang free from the lacy netting. His hands plumped the flesh, squeezing, caressing, then lifted her straining nipple to his mouth so he could suckle the tender nub of flesh.

A jolt of sexual longing swept through Paige, rendering her breathless.

Josh charted a path of wet kisses down her belly, bathed her navel with his tongue, while dragging her panties down her legs. He nudged her thighs apart, wasting no time in taking her deeply, carnally, with his mouth and tongue. She sucked in a breath and dug her fingers into his hair as her knees threatened to buckle. His tongue flicked, teased, stroked her slowly, sensually, drawing out the incredible pleasure until it became too intense to bear.

He pushed her over the edge and she soared, climaxing with a low, keening cry she couldn't hold back. Tremors rippled through her body, and he carried her the entire way.

For the briefest moment he left her, opening the nightstand drawer and groping for something inside—a condom, she realized in a dazed fog as she watched him tear open the foil pack and roll the protection onto his erection.

He glanced at her, his chest rising and falling, his gaze dark with unquenched passion, yet tinged with hesitancy, too. He made no move to reach for her, leaving the next decision up to her.

Unhooking her bra, she let it fall to the floor, then stepped toward him. Her palms pressed against his chest, guided him back until his legs hit the edge of the mattress. She followed him down onto the bed, straddled his hips, accepted the fullness of him and rode him. His hands were everywhere, fondling her breasts, rubbing her thighs, clutching her hips so he could drive deeper....

With a low, masculine growl, he rolled, pinning her beneath him, so they were face-to-face. Heart to beating heart.

She touched his jaw, stared into his eyes. "I love you, Josh," she whispered, the words slipping out of their own accord. She didn't regret saying them, couldn't, not when tonight held so many uncertainties, so many risks.

"I know," was all he said, then lowered his head and kissed her sweetly, tenderly.

He made love to her with exquisite slowness, extending their time together for as long as possible. Eventually, his measured thrusts gained momentum. Wrapping her legs around his waist, she lifted her hips, urging him deeper, urging him to fill the darkest part of her soul. Languid strokes became harder, quicker, a succession of rhythmic lunges that made him groan and shudder and finally reach his own powerful orgasm.

Minutes later, when he finally recovered, he lifted up on his forearms to stare down at her, and brushed away tendrils of hair from her face with his fingers. A gentle smile curved his mouth, but an awesome sadness filled his eyes. "How's that headache of yours?"

She laughed when all she wanted to do was cry. "Cured," she said, wishing there was as simple a remedy for the consuming ache in her heart.

11

"I HOPE VICTOR doesn't penalize for tardiness," Paige murmured wryly as she and Josh made their way along the tiled walkway leading back to the mansion. The sun was setting behind them, spreading a glorious array of fiery colors across the sky. Carranza's big house loomed in front of them, foreboding and imposing, causing an uneasy shiver to race through her.

"We're fashionably late," Josh stated, giving the hand tucked in his a squeeze. "And considering Carranza's 'amenities' are at fault, I'm sure he won't hold us accountable."

Her skin flushed at his blatant reminder of how they'd spent the afternoon—how they'd made good use of those condoms stashed in the nightstand. Her face warmed even more when she realized the undercover officers planted around the estate were privy to their intimate conversation, via the wireless listening devices they wore.

After making love the first time, Josh had pulled her into his arms and ordered her to rest. Safe in his embrace, she'd dozed off, only to wake an hour later to his hands caressing her breasts and his warm, damp breath on her neck. Instinctively, her body came alive for him, and she turned toward the heat he generated, her legs automatically parting for him to slide in between. He loved her in more ways then she could ever have imagined, each time taking her higher, satisfying a hunger that had been building for years.

They'd showered together, scrubbing each other's backs, chests, bellies, thighs, and other tender, sensitive areas. The water steamed, Josh's hands glided over slick skin, and his mouth and tongue started the feverish need again. This time was desperate and a little rough as he took her against the tiled shower wall, his hips pumping repeatedly, frantically, as she arched to meet his deep thrusts. His mouth was just as bruising, marking her in the most primitive sense. His eyes glowed hotly, and his hands gripped her buttocks, pushing, pulling, establishing a relentless sensual slide that elicited those strong, feminine contractions from the depths of her womb. And then he came, head thrown back, eyes closed, a low, ragged groan ripping from his chest.

Satiated, he'd slid to his knees, taking her with him so she straddled his hips and their bodies remained joined. The water beat down on his back, drizzling over them like rain. They kissed and touched, loath to separate. Finally, the water grew chilled, forcing them to face the inevitable.

They dressed, she in a long black velvet gown that left her shoulders bare to display the dazzling Ivanov necklace, and Josh in the tuxedo he'd rented for the weekend. He'd secured his revolver beneath his pant leg at his ankle, then silently tended to Paige's means of self-defense. Slipping his hand into the sexy slit of her dress that reached to just above the knee, he strapped a small holster around her thigh to hold her derringer. His fingers had lingered, stroking her skin, as if one last touch would sustain him for the rest of his life.

"Carranza is expecting so many people, I'm sure we

can slip in unnoticed," Josh said as they neared the elegant mansion.

His deep, reassuring voice dissolved the intimate thoughts flitting through Paige's mind. She nodded, her gaze on Carranza's sprawling manor, her throat too tight to speak. Lights glittered from the windows and lilting music drifted out the second-story balcony doors. Her stomach churned with apprehension and she wished the awful sensation away. She had to remain calm and focused—emotional strength would carry her through this ordeal. She realized that this man by her side gave her that courage.

About ten yards away from the back entrance to the mansion, Josh stopped and abruptly pulled her into his arms, kissing her one last time. She returned the embrace, uncaring who witnessed the exchange. His heart beat rapidly beneath the palm she pressed to his chest, matching the cadence of her own pulse.

He lifted his mouth and stared down at her, his eyes soft and infinitely tender. Warm fingers traced the outline of the Ivanov necklace to where it formed a V near her cleavage. She'd worn her hair up, and a slight breeze tickled the fine hairs at the back of her neck.

"You look beautiful," he murmured.

She managed a smile and brushed back a lock of dark hair that had fallen over his brow. "You don't look so bad yourself."

He cocked his head and offered her his arm. "Shall we?"

Drawing a deep fortifying breath, she nodded and looped her hand through his forearm. He led the way inside, following the stream of people heading up a spiral staircase to the second level of the mansion, a section of which was filled with round tables draped in fine linen, and set with gleaming silver and gold-rimmed china. A huge parquet dance floor dominated the other half of the ballroom.

The place was overflowing with men in black tuxedos and custom-made suits, and women dressed in elegant gowns and fabulous glittering jewels. Paige's necklace was by far the most stunning, the diamonds and emeralds winking under the light the crystal chandelier cast off. Men nodded as she and Josh mingled, and women stared, their gazes moving from the Ivanov piece to her face, then on to Josh, where their smiles turned decidedly friendly. Josh smiled back, though the possessive way he touched her made it more than clear that his interest was captured solely by her.

Paige felt like a fraud in this elite gathering, and very uncomfortable. The necklace hung like a hundred-pound weight around her throat, and she tried not to think about the compact gun pressed so snugly against her thigh.

Jacketed waiters passed with trays of champagne and appetizers, making brief eye contact with Josh and leaving Paige to wonder if they were Metro-Dade officers. Josh retrieved two crystal goblets of the fizzing liquid and handed one to her, for appearances' sake, she assumed. Not daring to taste any more than a few drops on her tongue, she pretended to sip the bubbling drink. She wanted nothing to cloud her judgment or reflexes.

A five-piece band played jazz music, laughter filled the room, and Paige struggled to keep at bay the anxiety creeping over her. She wanted this confrontation over and done with, but knew Carranza would pursue the necklace in his own time. She couldn't imagine how he would confiscate the Ivanov piece with so many people around to witness an exchange. According to Reynolds's plan, she wasn't to take the necklace off, but had been instructed to bait him so he'd be forced to resort to extreme measures that would put him in a position to be prosecuted.

"Ah, there you are, Paige." Carranza's smooth voice drifted from behind them. "I've been looking for you."

Paige's heart leapt. Lifting her lips in a semblance of a smile, she and Josh turned to find Victor and a shorter man with a severely receding hairline standing beside him. Both were dressed in black tuxedos, and Paige decided the sinister color suited them.

Carranza's gaze touched on the necklace, then traveled up to meet her eyes. "I take it your headache is gone?"

"Yes, I feel much better." Most likely, if he'd bugged the room, he knew exactly how she and Josh had spent the afternoon—living up to the pretense of lovers. His congenial expression, however, didn't give away a thing.

"Good." Picking up her hand, he patted it affectionately. Her skin crawled, and she resisted the urge to jerk her fingers from his. "It would be a shame if you didn't enjoy the evening because you weren't feeling well." Releasing her hand, he inclined his head toward Josh. "Mr. Bennett, are you enjoying yourself?"

"Immensely." Josh saluted Carranza with his glass of champagne and smiled indulgently. "The amenities are outstanding."

If their performance hadn't been so crucial, Paige would have elbowed Josh in the ribs for that remark.

Carranza stared at Josh for a long moment, and though he smiled, there was a sudden dark glint in his eyes that made Paige nervous. Then he turned toward the older man beside him. "Paige, I'd like you to meet

Alfred, my personal appraiser. Alfred, this is Paige Montgomery, proprietress of the Wild Rose, the boutique I expressed an interest in for Bridget."

"It's a pleasure." Alfred shook her hand, then Josh's, his beady gaze drawn to the diamonds and emeralds draped over her throat. "The necklace is exquisite," he agreed, a dark brow rising. "I can see why Bridget wants it for herself."

"She's been pouting ever since she saw it in a portrait Paige has hanging in her boutique." A waiter passed with a tray of appetizers, which they all declined. Carranza glanced back at Paige. "Would you mind if Alfred has a closer look at your necklace?"

She smiled sweetly and lightly touched the jewels. "I'd rather not take it off."

Carranza didn't look pleased by her refusal, but quickly covered up his irritation and offered an alternate suggestion. "Very well, he can give it a quick appraisal while you're wearing it."

His audacity shouldn't have surprised her, and as much as she wanted to deny his request so she didn't have to endure his appraiser groping the necklace and her neck, she had no justifiable reason to do so.

Alfred lifted a jeweler's loupe to his eye, and took hold of the diamond and emeralds to inspect them. Paige stiffened as his cold fingers brushed her skin, and tried desperately not to shudder in revulsion. Josh stood beside her, looking appropriately bored.

Finally, Alfred released the necklace and stepped back, giving Carranza a slight nod. "It's a very fine piece," he declared.

A satisfied smile touched Victor's mouth. His narrowed gaze scanned the crowd of people, and finding Bridget holding court amongst a cluster of men, he motioned for her. She glided toward them, her sleek body wrapped in a black sheath that displayed every curve.

She nodded to Paige, gave Josh a sultry once-over, then glanced up at Carranza.

Victor smiled at her. "Pussycat, are you sure this is the necklace you want?"

She eyed the diamonds and emeralds, her full lips pursing petulantly. "I'm sure. Whatever it costs, I want this original, *not* a duplication."

"Very well." Carranza released a long-suffering sigh, then glanced back at Paige. "Perhaps later this evening we can discuss a fair price for the necklace?"

Paige laughed lightly, a chuckle that sounded strained to her own ears, and forced the reply Josh had rehearsed with her. "Actually, I've had other inquiries about the necklace. I heard it was part of the Ivanov collection and I'm not sure I want to part with it." She caressed the smooth jewels and smiled. "After all, it does have a certain sentimental value attached to it."

A muscle in Carranza's jaw twitched, and something dark and dangerous glittered in his eyes. "I hope you'll reconsider."

She gave a noncommittal shrug. "Maybe it would be best for Bridget to find another emerald-and-diamond necklace that is more...*attainable*."

Bridget's gaze sparked with a flash of fury that sent a touch of fear skittering along Paige's spine. Carranza, too, looked none too happy with her unwillingness to give them what they wanted. Obviously, they hadn't planned on her not cooperating.

To Paige's immense relief, dinner was announced, interrupting the tense moment. Obviously displeased, Carranza excused himself, and flanked by Bridget and Alfred, headed toward the dining area.

"Well, he's certainly been baited," Paige commented, leaning close to Josh as they wended their way to the table they'd been assigned to.

He pulled out a chair for her to sit. "We'll see what happens," he murmured, then took the seat next to her.

They spent the next hour dining on a fabulous five-course meal. Josh ate his dinner with gusto, but Paige pushed her food around on her plate, knowing her churning stomach would never be able to digest any of the rich entrées. Instead, she nibbled on her bread and consumed three glasses of water, hoping that bland diet would settle her anxiety. They conversed politely with the couples seated at their table, but Paige remembered little of what they'd discussed.

After dinner, she and Josh danced, mingled and went out onto the balcony for fresh air, all the while waiting and wondering what Carranza had planned next. Though they'd spoken at intervals during the party, Carranza had made no more mention of his interest in the Ivanov necklace. He was again pleasant and charming. If she hadn't known better, she would have thought he'd accepted her refusal to sell him the piece.

The night wore on. People gradually retired for the evening, and Paige grew weary, too. She hated to think that all the preparation for this weekend would be for nothing—she also didn't want to leave Miami with Carranza still on the loose, and Josh in the midst of the danger surrounding the case.

Out on the dance floor, Josh held her securely as they moved to a slow ballad, along with several other couples still enjoying the evening's festivities. With every shift of her body against Josh's, she became increasingly aware of the uncomfortable pressure low in her belly—nature had been calling for the past two hours.

"Josh, I really have to go to the ladies' room," she said, more urgently than the other two times she'd made the same request.

He frowned, the hand resting at the base of her spine tightening perceptively. "Can't you hold it a little while longer?"

If the situation hadn't become so dire, she would have laughed. "No," she groaned, her frustration coming through in the tone of her voice. "Between the three glasses of water I drank during dinner and the soda I just finished, my bladder is going to explode if I don't empty it. And soon." Glancing around the ballroom, she found Carranza. "Victor and Bridget are busy talking to that group of people. You keep an eye on them, and I'll be back in less than two minutes," she suggested, knowing how odd it would look for Josh to accompany her to the rest room and stand guard.

Hesitant emotions entered his gaze. He clearly didn't want her out of his sight, not even to take care of a necessity.

"Josh, I'm wired," she reminded him in a low voice. "There'll be two dozen men in that rest room with me."

An amused smile kicked up the corner of his mouth. "You're right," he conceded, casting a glance toward the hired bartender. The man gave a barely discernible nod to indicate he'd heard them.

Reluctantly, Josh let her go, and she headed toward a hallway that took her out of Josh's line of vision and led to a rest room. Thankfully, it was unoccupied. Locking the door behind her, she took care of business as quickly as possible. While washing her hands, she glimpsed her reflection. She looked pale and tired, though the Ivanov necklace sparkled with a life of its own. She wondered how something so beautiful and extraordinary could be the root of so much evil and greed.

Somebody tested the doorknob, pulling her out of her idle musings. She realized she'd taken at least five minutes instead of the two she'd promised Josh, and that he was probably growing frantic with worry.

"I'll be just a second," she called to the person on the other side of the door as she tucked back a stray strand of hair that had escaped her chignon. She stifled a yawn and straightened her dress, thinking she and Josh ought to call it a night, since Carranza didn't seem inclined to make a move for the necklace that evening.

With that thought on her weary mind, she exited the rest room and collided with a solid wall of muscle that caused her to take a step back to steady herself. Startled, she glanced up, expecting Josh, but found herself staring at a middle-aged man with a deep, two-inch scar along his cheek. He was dressed in the requisite black, his long ebony hair pulled back and secured at the back of his neck with a thin leather strap.

"I'm sorry," she said, suddenly realizing how quiet the hallway was, and that they were alone, just the two of them. "I should have been paying better attention to where I was going." She attempted to step around him.

He blocked her path, large and immobile. Foreboding snaked along the surface of her skin and kicked up the adrenaline in her system. He smiled, the gesture as dark and evil as his black eyes. Full-fledged terror gripped her. Every instinct she possessed screamed at her to bolt, but he anticipated her intent.

He grasped her arm so brutally, she sucked in a sharp breath, cutting off the protest forming on her lips. Before she could recover from that painful assault, he forcefully guided her down the hallway, away from the ballroom.

"Make a sound and you're dead," he informed her, his tone as feral as his threatening words.

SITTING AT their dinner table while he waited for Paige to return from the ladies' room, Josh casually glanced at his watch for the seventh time in as many minutes.

He had a clear view of the corridor that led to the rest room, and no one had entered or exited from that direction since Paige. Tension tightened the cords in his neck and bunched the muscles along his shoulders. When another minute crept by with no sign of Paige, he grew even more restless, his eyes shifting from the hallway to Carranza and back again, his mind flipping through a multitude of scenarios—none of which were pleasant.

A young man Josh had seen with Carranza throughout the night approached Victor, and Josh watched as they exchanged words. Carranza's expression took on a cold, calculating presence, and he nodded to his messenger. Excusing himself from the group he'd been visiting with, Carranza then exited the ballroom through the main entrance.

The fact that Carranza had departed in the opposite direction to where Paige had gone did little to reassure Josh. His gut twisted with an awful premonition. A discreet but urgent nod from the bartender confirmed his suspicions.

Something had happened to Paige, and she was in trouble.

Forcing a calm he was hard-pressed to maintain, Josh headed toward the brass-and-mahogany bar. He waited anxiously for the couple in front of him to order and receive their drinks, then leave to mingle. Once he was alone with the bartender, Josh stepped closer to the brass railing, careful not to make eye contact with the undercover officer on the opposite side of the bar. The other man kept busy as well, clearing the empty glasses a waiter had delivered.

"I'll take a club soda," Josh said, aware that Bridget was keeping an eye on him from across the room.

The bartender set a glass with ice on the pour pad and used a spigot to fill it with the carbonated liquid. "Study. West wing. First level."

The officer's words were low and clipped, but Josh latched on to each one, knowing that somehow, between the network of other undercover officers planted around the estate, and any information or clues Paige might have been able to utter while being abducted, they'd managed to determine her location.

This was it, he realized. The moment they'd planned for.

Josh didn't know the layout of the mansion, could only go by the bartender's brief, vague directions. He had to get to the first landing, but how? Bridget had moved to talk to a small gathering of people near the entrance of the ballroom and would no doubt waylay him should he attempt to leave. A glance toward the corridor leading to the rest room nixed the idea of finding the same back stairway Paige had taken with her own personal guide. Two burly men dressed in black stood near that hallway like obedient rottweilers.

Feeling trapped, frustrated, and trying not to think about the fear Paige was experiencing, Josh searched for an alternate escape, and found only one. Taking his drink, he moved around the room, keeping an eye on Bridget. When a guest temporarily diverted her attention, he slipped out onto the balcony, startling the two women who stood outside, taking in the cool evening air.

So much for disappearing unnoticed. Knowing his choices were limited, Josh nodded amicably at the pair, set his drink down on a glass-topped table, and climbed over the wrought-iron railing. One of the women gasped, while the other stared at him, both shocked at his behavior.

He grinned and winked, striving for a charm he was far from feeling. "If anybody should ask, you didn't see me," he said, hoping to buy himself time with their co-operation. Sliding down the railing, he gripped the ledge of the balcony, straightened his body, then dropped to the ground nearly ten feet below. Pain shot up his legs, but he gave it little thought—he hadn't broken any bones and that was all he cared about.

Drawing his weapon and crouching low, he made his way to the back entrance of the manor and slipped inside. All was quiet; Carranza's staff was upstairs, attending the party. Heading toward the west wing, he negotiated what seemed like a maze of hallways. He checked every room he passed, murmuring his location as he moved along so he'd have backup when he needed it. Time seemed to drag as he stealthily searched the lower level of the mansion, listening for sounds and voices behind closed doors. Sweat beaded his brow and his heart pumped frantically in his chest when each room turned up dark and empty.

Where in the hell was she?

WHERE IN THE HELL was he?

Paige swallowed the panic rising in her throat, desperate not to succumb to the blinding terror hovering just below the facade of calm she'd managed to maintain in Carranza's and his thug's presence.

With a firm push between her shoulder blades, the thug nudged her deeper into the study, toward the large marble-topped desk Carranza stood behind. The room smelled of leather, fine tobacco and money. The combination of odors made Paige's stomach clench; the insidious glimmer in Carranza's gaze made her entire body tremble.

She lifted her chin, refusing to cower. "I don't appreciate being manhandled by the hired help."

Carranza appeared amused. "If you hadn't been so difficult about parting with the necklace, none of this would have been necessary." Hands clasped behind his back, he circled the desk and slowly approached her. "I would have been happy to compensate you a few thousand dollars for the necklace, and we could have parted without any complications. Unfortunately, you've forced me to take a more drastic approach."

She flinched when he reached out to unclasp the necklace, shuddered in revulsion when his fingers brushed along her neck. She thought about using the gun strapped to her thigh, but with Carranza in front of her and the thug behind her, she knew she was outnumbered and outmuscled.

So, she endured Carranza's touch, grateful when he finally pulled his hands away from her body. His expression turned euphoric as he gazed at the diamonds and emeralds in his hand, his eyes taking on a glimmer of greedy excitement. Even his breathing changed as he stroked the glittering jewels, growing deep, eager, almost aroused.

She watched him walk back behind his desk, lift a painting from the wall, and open the safe behind it. Lifting a black-velvet-lined tray from the vault, he placed it on his desk. Rubies, sapphires, diamonds and an assortment of other jewels sparkled in the light—a heap of treasures Paige suspected had been pilfered, just as the Ivanov necklace had been.

"Ahh, now my collection is complete," he murmured ecstatically, more to himself than anybody else in the room.

She broke out in a cold sweat, shivering despite the warmth of the room. Where was Josh? she wondered desperately. She'd dropped as many clues as to her whereabouts as she possibly could without being obvious. Had something gone wrong?

Carranza glanced up at her, regret clouding the exuberant light in his eyes. "I really do apologize that things have to end this way, Mrs. Montgomery. But there's something about you I don't trust, just like that husband of yours."

The reference to Anthony and his deception that had resulted in this entire mess pushed Paige to the brink of hysteria. Carranza wasn't a stupid man—had he figured out that he'd been set up?

His gaze transferred to the thug behind her. "Get rid of her and Bennett," he ordered ruthlessly. "And make it look like an accident."

Surely her wireless microphone had transmitted that, she thought deliriously. She prayed help came, and soon, before there was no one left to save!

The man behind her grabbed her upper arm, and she struggled to free herself of his punishing grip. With little effort, he twisted her arm behind her back, and she cried out as white-hot pain electrified the nerve endings along her arm and shoulders, momentarily paralyzing her. She arched to accommodate the pressure, but h seemed to take great pleasure in tormenting her. With the threat of her limb snapping, she was forced to comply when he shoved her forward, toward the study's entrance.

The man opened the door, only to be greeted by Josh, who stood two feet away with his revolver aimed at the thug's head.

Worry and relief flashed across Josh's features, then were replaced by grim determination. "Let her go," he ordered, his tone low and fierce.

Ignoring his command, the man tightened his hold and slowly backed into the study, keeping Paige positioned in front of him as a shield. Josh moved forward, following him, the barrel of his gun sighted and steady.

"How convenient of you to join us," Carranza said insolently, capturing Josh's attention and forcing him to choose between the lesser of two evils.

His gun automatically swung toward Carranza, who stood behind his desk, unflinching, and without a weapon to defend himself. "The party's over, Carranza," Josh said, positioning himself with his back to the wall. "Tell your man to let her go."

Carranza lifted a brow and smiled. "I don't think so."

In that instant, the thug drew a pistol from his waistband, banded an arm around Paige's waist and pointed the barrel at her temple.

A fearful whimper escaped her dry throat.

Josh whirled and trained his gun on the thug, his expression furious, though Paige could detect his frustration, too. The man behind her laughed menacingly, knowing full well he had Josh in a stalemate. Josh knew it, too.

Very calmly, Carranza said, "I suggest you put the gun down, or watch your lover die."

"Josh, no," she countered in a shaky whisper. If he surrendered his weapon, he would die, she knew. They were going to die regardless, according to Carranza's plan.

He wavered, his jaw clenching. She suspected he was stalling for time, praying as she was for their backup to arrive.

"Do it now," Carranza ordered impatiently.

Reluctantly, Josh slowly lowered his gun to the floor. Tears burned the back of Paige's eyes when she realized that he was sacrificing his own life for hers.

If she didn't do something, and fast, once he let go of his weapon, they were both going to end up dead. Hating what she was about to do, but knowing her options were limited, she deliberately stumbled to the side, catching the thug behind her off guard. He swore and fought to support both of them so they didn't completely lose their balance. Taking advantage of the distraction, she reached inside the slit in her dress, grabbed the derringer from its holster and planted the barrel against the thug's belly. Squeezing her eyes shut, she pulled the trigger, moaning as the room exploded with sound. The man behind her automatically released her, sucking in a wheezing breath as he crumpled to the floor. The gun in his hand skittered across the carpet out of reach.

Josh recovered his gun, but Carranza had retrieved his own weapon from his desk drawer, and their barrels sighted each other at the exact same moment. Neither hesitated to squeeze the trigger.

Two gunshots reverberated in the study, the blast echoing like cannons. In horrible slow motion, Paige watched as Josh stumbled back, his eyes wide as h clutched his chest, a harsh moan of pain escaping him before he finally collapsed to the floor.

"Nooooo!" she screamed, dropping her own weapon to rush to his side as all hell seemed to break loose around her. Armed men flooded the room, barking orders and swarming the area. They could have been Carranza's cohorts for all she cared—her only concern was with Josh and his injury.

On her hands and knees on the carpet, she pushed back his tuxedo jacket, moaning pitifully when she saw the dark, spreading stain of blood on his white shirt. His eyes were closed, his body limp, his expression lax—she feared the absolute worst.

She touched his cheek, willing him to live. "Damn you, Josh, don't you dare leave me," she said in a choked whisper as hot tears streamed down her face. "After everything we've been through, I won't let you leave me!"

12

HE WAS HAVING the most wonderful dream. He was being cared for by an angel with a sweet, husky voice, and soft, cool hands that caressed his brow, making him momentarily forget the searing heat in his shoulder. Gentle lips brushed his cheek. That same tempting voice whispered encouraging words in his ear.

I love you, Josh Marchiano.

Ahh, maybe he was in Heaven. Yeah, that had to be it.

He tried to move toward that cajoling voice, that delectable feminine scent that overrode more antiseptic smells, and moaned as a shaft of pain ripped along his chest and arm. He wouldn't have thought he'd feel such burning discomfort in Heaven. Soothing fingers fluttered along his good shoulder—an angel, maybe?—distracting him from the gnawing ache on his left side.

"Come on, Marchiano, I expect you to pull through this like the tough guy you are."

No, definitely not an angel, unless they were extremely bossy.

He forced his eyes to open, his gaze falling on the woman sitting next to him on the edge of the narrow hospital bed.

Paige.

He'd thought he'd never see her again. When he'd felt Carranza's bullet rip through his flesh, before darkness had obliterated his mind, he'd had the fleeting thought that he'd failed her, just as Anthony had. That Carranza or one of his men would kill her, and he'd been the one to put her in such a dangerous situation. And he'd hated himself for that. Hated that he'd risked her life, and ultimately proved that he was no better than her husband had been.

But she was very much alive, and he was grateful enough for that huge blessing to know that he had to let her go, set her free.

She wore no makeup, and she'd clipped her rich auburn hair back from her pale face, which emphasized the dark crescents beneath her eyes. The depths of those striking green eyes were filled with tenderness, exhaustion and a determination that seemed soul-deep. Despite appearing fatigued and worried, she looked absolutely beautiful—as close to an angel as he would have ever wanted.

But she wasn't his to keep confined, no matter how much he loved her. He realized that, accepted it, no matter how painful losing her would be.

"Hi," he rasped, his throat dry and scratchy.

She smiled, a multitude of emotions shimmering in her eyes. "Hi, yourself, tough guy," she said, her voice sounding as tight as his own had. "We've been waiting for you to wake up."

His gaze scanned the small hospital room, finding it empty except for them. "We?"

"Me. Your parents. Your brothers and sisters. The entire gang." Picking up the cup of water on a nearby tray, she slipped the straw between his lips so he could take a drink. "They're in the lounge, but if you don't mind, I want you for myself for a few minutes before the cavalry arrives."

Josh knew once his family swooped in, he and Paige wouldn't have any time alone. Selfish as it might be, he wanted every moment alone with Paige that he could get. Too soon, she'd be gone, and he'd only have memories to remember her by.

"What day is it?" he asked, trying to orient himself.

She smiled. "It's Monday morning."

He frowned. "I lost a day somewhere." He tried to think back, but his mind wouldn't cooperate. He caught images, but nothing solid. "What happened?"

"You were shot in the shoulder Saturday night at Carranza's estate, and knocked unconscious," she told him, gently smoothing the blanket over his chest. "You were flown to the hospital for surgery and given enough painkillers to keep you sedated for the past twenty-four hours. But you came through just fine. The doctor said you'll be back to work within a few months."

The last thing he wanted to think about was work. "What happened to Carranza?"

"He's dead," she said quietly. "Your aim was more accurate than his. Seconds after you were shot, the undercover officers arrived. Everyone involved in the jewel-smuggling ring was arrested, and they found enough evidence to make a conviction stick."

"Good." Josh nodded, pleased that the undercover operation had been successful and a band of criminals would be put away for a very long time. Maybe, as a result, Paige could put that nightmarish part of her past to rest, too.

He shifted to find a more comfortable position, and grimaced as his upper body protested the slightest movement. Paige immediately stood and fussed over him, using the remote control to lift his mattress until he sat up in a relaxed, reclining position. She fluffed his pillows, gave him more cold water to drink and rearranged the light blanket around his waist.

"Ummm, I could get used to this," he teased.

She abruptly stopped her pampering, suddenly appearing nervous. He wondered if his comment had been too personal, too full of the intimation that he wanted her to stay and take care of him. He did want that, more than his next breath, but he'd already made the decision to set her free and he wouldn't renege on that promise. He'd love her forever, but she deserved to be happy—even if that meant letting her live her own life in Connecticut with her family, thousands of miles away from him.

"How are you feeling?" she asked, propping her hip on the edge of the mattress once again, her gaze concerned, but anxious, too.

"A little uncomfortable with the pain in my shoulder, and a whole lot happy to be alive." He reached for her hand, twining his fingers with hers. "And even happier to see that you're okay. No one hurt you?"

She shook her head. "A few bruises, but nothing that won't heal. Because of you, I'm fine."

He balked at that. "I can't take all the credit, Paige. I know how much you hate guns, and what you did was incredibly brave. I'm so proud of you. You saved both of our lives." More hesitantly, he added, "And now that the case is over, you're free to go back home."

He thought she'd be relieved, but the panic that filled her expression confused him.

"I thought I'd lost you," she whispered, moisture glittering in her incredible green eyes. "And when I saw all that blood on your shirt, all I could think was that if you died, so would I."

A reassuring smile formed on his lips. "As you can see, I'm fine." Reaching up, he gently brushed away a tear that trailed down her smooth cheek. "You're one of the most courageous women I know."

Paige bit her trembling bottom lip, finding it difficult to accept Josh's praise when she'd come to a stunning conclusion while waiting for him to awaken after his surgery. "I'm a coward," she blurted.

He laughed, then groaned as his expression of amusement caused him discomfort. "What in the world makes you think you're a coward?"

She drew a deep, shaky breath. "Because I'm afraid—"

"You had every right to be afraid, sweetheart," he interrupted, his tone fierce, but gentle. "You were in a life-threatening situation."

He'd misunderstood her. Frustrated, she struggled to put her emotions into words and not fumble her chances with Josh in the process. "I'm afraid of losing you, Josh. What happened at Carranza's estate made me realize that. Seeing you near death put things into very clear perspective." He opened his mouth to say something but she pressed three fingers to his lips, imploring him to be quiet and just listen to her.

"My marriage to Anthony was a sham. You know that as well as I do," she went on, realizing that part of her past wasn't nearly as painful as it once had been. "And because of your profession, I feared that a life with you would be just as complicated. But you know what? Despite what you do for a living, you're nothing like Anthony. In my heart, I always knew that, but admitting it was something else. What you did for me this weekend forced me to face that realization."

His expression turned quizzical. "What did I do?" he murmured behind the press of her fingers.

"You gave your life to protect mine."

He bristled indignantly. "Protecting you was my job."

"Shut up, Marchiano, I'm talking," she ordered gently. "While Anthony endangered my life, you were willing to sacrifice yours for me. I don't think Anthony would have done that."

He didn't refute her claim. They both knew that Anthony had been too caught up in his own selfish desires to think of anyone but himself.

"You're a good, honorable man, Josh." More so than Anthony had ever been. Those honest values made all the difference in the world. "And you're willing to let me go, despite how much you love me."

"It's what you want," he said simply.

Her heart swelled at what he was willing to sacrifice for her, despite his own misery. "It's what I *thought* I wanted, because I was so wrapped up in the pain of my marriage to Anthony. His betrayal. His deception. And then I thought of all the times you were there for me when Anthony wasn't. How you so selflessly gave of yourself when I had no one to turn to. You've become my best friend, Josh, and I do love you."

"Ah, Paige," he groaned, the sound somewhere between pleasure and torment.

Emotion gathered in the back of her throat. "I can't imagine my life without you." The words were whispered, but she knew he heard them clearly.

He swallowed thickly. "We'll call each other," he rasped. "And I can visit you in Connecticut."

She shook her head. Darn man, he just didn't seem to comprehend what she was struggling to say. Then again, she'd given him no reason to hope for a future together. "I...I want more than just occasional phone calls and visits."

He went very still, watching her.

Exasperated, she said, "I want to marry you, Marchiano."

He stared, disbelief clashing with the hope she saw reflected in his gaze.

"I want to have your babies," she whispered.

His eyes glowed with pleasure, but was quickly eclipsed by caution. "Being a cop's wife isn't easy," he said gruffly. "We've talked about that."

"I know all about being a cop's wife, and I'll always worry about you. That won't change whether I'm here or in Connecticut." She took his face in between her hands, capturing his golden gaze with her own. "I believe in you, and I love you enough to put my future in your hands." She knew he would never jeopardize their commitment to each other as Anthony had. "I trust you, Josh," she said, giving him what she hadn't been able to give Anthony. "With my heart. My soul. My life. I'm hoping we can work on everything else together. Day by day."

With his good arm, he raised his hand and cupped the back of her head, pulling her down for a long, deep kiss that promised a lifetime of passion, commitment and love. She leaned into him, wanting to get as close as possible, but careful, too, of his bandaged shoulder.

Finally, he ended the kiss, but kept her close in his embrace. "I'll do everything within my power to make you happy, Paige."

Believing him was easy. "Yeah, I know you will." She smiled, her heart overflowing with joy. After the pain of the past two years, she felt she'd finally come home to a place where she belonged. It had nothing to do with the state or city in which she lived, and everything to do with the man who loved her so completely. "I was thinking maybe we could find a place in a quiet suburb just outside of Miami. A house with kid-proof furniture, an extra room for when your parents visit, and a big backyard."

A slow grin spread across his face. "We could do that."

She drew a slow, lazy pattern with her finger on his good arm. "And I'd like to keep the Wild Rose, but continue to have Pam manage it."

His eyes took on a wicked gleam. "That wouldn't be a bad idea, considering you're going to be busy with all the babies I plan to give you."

She laughed, the sound light and carefree. "I'm gonna hold you to that, Marchiano, just as soon as you get out of this place."

"Then I'm going to demand being discharged this afternoon." He waggled his brows at her. "Didn't you say something about it being a few months before I could return to work?"

She rolled her eyes. "I guess I'm going to have my hands full with you, huh?"

"Oh yeah," he murmured. "And then some."

Paige sighed as they indulged in another lengthy kiss that erased the pain of the past, and gave her the strength and courage to be this man's wife.

They had faith and love. The rest would come.

If you enjoyed what you just read,
then we've got an offer you can't resist!

Take 2 bestselling love stories FREE!

Plus get a FREE surprise gift!

Clip this page and mail it to Harlequin Reader Service®

IN U.S.A.	IN CANADA
3010 Walden Ave.	P.O. Box 609
P.O. Box 1867	Fort Erie, Ontario
Buffalo, N.Y. 14240-1867	L2A 5X3

YES! Please send me 2 free Harlequin Temptation® novels and my free surprise gift. Then send me 4 brand-new novels every month, which I will receive months before they're available in stores. In the U.S.A., bill me at the bargain price of $3.12 plus 25¢ delivery per book and applicable sales tax, if any*. In Canada, bill me at the bargain price of $3.57 plus 25¢ delivery per book and applicable taxes**. That's the complete price and a savings of over 10% off the cover prices—what a great deal! I understand that accepting the 2 free books and gift places me under no obligation ever to buy any books. I can always return a shipment and cancel at any time. Even if I never buy another book from Harlequin, the 2 free books and gift are mine to keep forever. So why not take us up on our invitation. You'll be glad you did!

142 HEN CNEV
342 HEN CNEW

Name _____ (PLEASE PRINT)

Address _____ Apt.# _____

City _____ State/Prov. _____ Zip/Postal Code _____

* Terms and prices subject to change without notice. Sales tax applicable in N.Y.
** Canadian residents will be charged applicable provincial taxes and GST.
  All orders subject to approval. Offer limited to one per household.
  ® are registered trademarks of Harlequin Enterprises Limited.

TEMP99   ©1998 Harlequin Enterprises Limited

COMING NEXT MONTH

#733 ONE WILD WEEKEND Rita Clay Estrada
Bachelor Auction

Buying time with renowned photographer Archer was
Melody Chase's last chance. She needed to know how to land a
man, and who better qualified to tell her than someone who
spent his life dealing with desirable women? The problem was,
Archer decided he wanted Melody for himself...for only one
wild weekend.

#734 SEXY AS SIN Meg Lacey

When Chastity Goodwin saw sexy Sin O'Connor roar up to her
door on a motorcycle, she knew she was in for a fight. No way
was this man going to willingly replace his black leather and
denim for a doublet and tights—not even for his brother's
wedding! But Sin was full of surprises. And willing to take off
his clothes...as long as Chastity did, too.

#735 WHILE HE WAS SLEEPING Carolyn Andrews
The Wrong Bed

Hopeless romantic Daisy Hanover wasn't looking forward to
her upcoming marriage of convenience. So when she discovered
a quaint country inn, boasting a bed that promised wedded bliss
to the couple who shared it, Daisy made arrangements for her
fiancé to meet her. After one night, Daisy definitely found bliss.
Only, the man in her bed *wasn't* her fiancé!

#736 BRAZEN Carly Phillips
Blaze

After agreeing to a loveless marriage, Samantha Reed decided
to run away for a week and experience a lifetime's worth of
passion—even if it was with a stranger! Sexy bartender
Ryan "Mac" Mackenzie seemed like the perfect man to love and
leave behind. Only, Mac wasn't a bartender—and he wasn't
letting Samantha go anywhere....